BEFORE T.
GE] ...

It was 6:40. am. Gemma slumped out of bed the way she always did. She forced her slippers on, kissed Esther on the cheek and went downstairs to make them both coffees. The tar coloured clouds offered no promise for

better days to come, and the rain always pissed it down. She wondered if it was ever going to bloody stop, and not just the rain.

To put it bluntly, Gemma couldn't stand work anymore. It was like taking a shit when you were constipated; you knew it was going to be painful when it was happening, but you were comforted by the knowledge that afterwards, it would be a relief.

After she made coffee, Gemma made her way back upstairs. She took caution with each step,

making sure she didn't spill any. Esther would have scolded her for it because she had ordered brand new carpets last week and of course, they were bright crème. Esther wore the trousers in their relationship and Gemma knew it. She didn't mind though; it was a small price to pay for being privileged enough to call this woman her fiancé.

"Two coffees. One for myself and one for the lady of the manor," Gemma said. She smirked and placed one mug down on a coaster by her side of the bed. She passed the other mug to Esther who took the handle reluctantly, rubbing her eyes and yawning inelegantly.

"Oh, your phone buzzed. I'm sorry I didn't pick it up, I was still half asleep."

Gemma grabbed her phone and unlocked it. There, on her screen. Big. Bold.

(5) MISSED CALLS – MICK.

"Oh, shit. It was Mick. Babe, why didn't you shout me?"

There was a moment of silence. Esther flicked through her diary, totally oblivious.

"Bet you don't know what today is?" she said, wide-eyed, accompanied by a widespread grin, which exposed her impeccable advert mouth.

Gemma didn't respond. Instead, her head was buried in her phone, her thumb swiping up and down, scrolling through her messages. Mick wouldn't have called at that time unless it was urgent. But then again, all the work Gemma did was urgent. That was also the thrill of it.

"Gem? What's going on?' Esther asked. She nudged Gemma's leg to get her attention, but this proved to be an exercise in futility. Once Gemma was

onto something, there was no breaking her concentration. She transformed into a predator, tracking down its prey. There was no chance of distraction.

Esther let out a long sigh. She got up, threw her dressing gown on the floor, crossed her arms and huffed in an attempt to get Gemma's attention. Still, she was in a world of her own.

Esther turned to another tactic, staring long and hard, waiting for Gemma's sudden realisation of her own ignorance. But of course, that didn't work either.

"Well, if you really want to know... today is our last chance to start a proper family," Esther said, failing in her attempt to stifle the breaking in her voice, "We're not getting any younger, you know? You're thirty-eight next year."

That did the trick.

In a flash, Gemma stopped swiping and dropped her phone, guilt hanging its weight on her features.

"Oh Est. I'm so... "

"Sorry? Yeah, thought you might use that one."

"Oh, come on babe. I've been so busy, I'm sorry."

"Just forget it. Not like you'll have trouble with that one is it?" Esther hissed, stormed off, wiping her eyes theatrically.

Before Gemma had a chance to save herself, her phone buzzed. It was Mick. She accepted the call, closing the bedroom door to avoid getting into any more trouble with Esther. That was the last thing she needed.

"Gem?" Mick said. His voice was always rough, each word sounding like a tyre scraping over gravel.

"Mick. Look, I'm really sorry abo- "

"Just get down to the station. It's urgent," he interrupted.

Gemma's stomach somersaulted.

"Code red?" Gemma asked, trying to drown out the volume of her pulse, loud and throbbing in both ears.

Mick's silence was an answer in itself.

After a few seconds, the call cut off.

When Gemma arrived at the Station as quickly as she could, she parked her car in the usual spot she'd parked it since the first day she started at the Station. She noticed Mick through the filthy smudged window of his office. He stood with his arms crossed, resting on his concrete chest. His head was bowed, his face stern.

"Ah, fucking brilliant, just what I need," Gemma muttered under her breath as she made her way inside.

As they caught eye contact, Mick gesticulated for her to make her way into the conference room.

Gemma nodded.

"Right, I'll just quickly ring Esther," she called over to Mick.

His lips tightened. He shook his head.

"I'm afraid you and lover girl will have to wait," he said.

Gemma appeared as though she had bitten into a lemon. On days when Mick was in a grumpy mood, he was the most impossible man in the world to reason with. Today was one of those days. It was an immediate indication to Gemma that this case was top priority.

"Well, I'll just go and get changed then... with your permission?"

"Five minutes tops. And be quick," Mick ordered, "oh and Gem? Less of the sarcasm, eh."

"Mardy git," Gemma said as she fumbled around for her locker key that annoyingly always fell right to bottom of her bag,

"Oh, for fuck sake," She said, opening the locker room door, her voice echoing.

"Giving you shit as well, is he?" A voice called from few lockers down.

Gemma gasped, jumped back into the locker door behind her and dropped her bag.

"Fuck, Scarlett! Scared me half to death."

Scarlett wandered over to Gemma in another one of her skin-tight black dresses. Tiny hairs from both sides of her head spilled out, along with other things that spilled out. She worked at the Café downstairs and sometimes cleaned the offices for extra money. She'd always been the talk of the office, especially with the younger men.

"Believe me Gem, I'm the least of your worries. I've heard about the case you're on," she said, not blinking once.

The silence between them impregnated the air. Gemma began to feel slightly uncomfortable, especially in such proximity to another woman who, she couldn't deny, embodied the metaphor of forbidden fruit.

"Well, I better be getting back to work. Thanks for the heads up," Gemma said, feigning a smile.

As Scarlett was about to leave, she turned back to Gemma and stood in the doorway for a few seconds.

"Good luck Gem. I'm sure you won't need it, but, good luck."

After Scarlett left, Gemma slumped her body against the locker. This was what she asked for. She knew deep in her gut that when she had agreed to do this job, these cases would come up. The cases that meant you wouldn't be getting very much sleep that night or for a few nights after.

Despite a level of anxiety, she felt like this might be *the* case. She thought it might have been the opportunity to show her talents, to apply her knowledge, to really impress Mick and get her big break. She'd done some great work before on previous cases, but this felt different. She saw the expression on Mick's face. From that, she knew. The mental weight of it was far heavier.

No matter how hard she tried to masque it though, no matter how much she had achieved in her career thus far, when it came down to it when she worked on cases like this, she was still that scared little girl. She was that innocent young thing with her life ahead of her, looking after her troubled Mother, paralysed with fear in her bedroom, anticipating the next beating she witnessed.

That same vulnerability was beginning to make an unwanted return. In those days during her adolescence, she had felt helpless. This only perpetuated as the years went on. That was until she met Esther, not too long after the dreaded news of her Mother's passing.

TOBY'S REVENGE

It was only when Gemma went for what she convinced herself was a one-off drink, that her life unexpectedly changed forever.

BEFORE THE MURDER

ESTHER

She did not just walk in when Esther arrived at Oakley Green. She strutted, into a small dingy pub called The Red Hen, located at the far end of Oakley Green. She wore a large silver Vivienne Westwood necklace and matching earrings. Her dress was Fred Perry, black, simple and elegant. Her shoes were Christian Louboutin's, heels fierce and striking, like her features. She naturally had that kind of glow that people paid obscene prices to achieve.

Once she and Gemma were acquainted at the bar, she had told her that she had recently just moved to the area, and was in all honesty, without a plan. She had no friends in the town, no family. Originally from Chelsea in London, she'd travelled to France on a gap year after studying Interior Design at UAL.

She wanted to play her cards right, the winning card being, I'm-a-young-attractive-helpless-woman-with-nowhere-to-go card. Someone here was bound to fall for it. After that, Gemma would be putty in her hands.

The Red Hen was your bog-standard cottage, nothing exceptional. It had been renovated into a place where people got pissed, like all derelict buildings no one knows what to do with. There were copious amounts of Ivy plants winding their way around the wooden pillars that stood before the front entrance. Esther imagined herself to be the Ivy, wrapping herself around Gemma.

Over the sea of rowdy leather-lunged men, chanting at the television screen which was showing the latest football game. Leeds vs West Bromwich Albion, Esther tried to speak with Gemma but had to shout at times.

TOBY'S REVENGE

Gemma was a perfect target in many ways. She was depressed, slumped over a large glass of Merlot almost bigger than her head, her fingers, circling the rim. Esther watched intently, concentrating on Gemma and Gemma only. It felt like for a few seconds, all noise in the room had faded. It was just them.

"Is it always this loud in here?" Esther asked, flicking her hair in Gemma's face purposefully to waft the scent of her perfume in her face.

Gemma sat up slowly and looked around, her face reddened, partly due to the sight of Esther and undeniably due to the wine.

Esther smiled for longer than she should have. She widened her eyes, raised her eyebrows and ensured that her best features were amplified.

Gemma appeared to be in complete shock, yet flattered.

She's probably never been approached by an attractive woman before, Esther thought to herself as she drank in Gemma's features. Shaven platinum blonde hair with a gelled quiff, puffy eyes, the dullest shade of brown, a shoestring mouth and an unpleasant looking nose that unfortunately took up most of her face. *She will do, her hair isn't that bad, I can deal with it*, Esther said to herself, smirking.

As the night went on, Esther could feel Gemma wanting to know more. Naturally, the more she found out, the more she wanted to know. But she couldn't know too much. Esther had to remain cautious, so as not to spill any information about her past. She had to stick to the story of who she was now. There was no room for slip-ups.

"What's a woman like you doing here in this quaint little town then?" Gemma asked, trying to disguise the fact she was pissed by over-pronouncing each word.

Esther flicked her hair back, laughing again.

"Well, whatever could you mean? A woman like me?"

Gemma flushed a deeper red, putting the Merlot to shame. It was so very *easy* to flatter her and Esther enjoyed every second of it, filling Gemma's mind up with this elaborate lie of who she was and why she was here.

"Oh, forgive me, I've had a few. I just couldn't help but notice how you're dressed. You know, all the designer gear you have on. Someone like you wouldn't really be in these parts. You must be married to a rich husband or something?" Gemma asked.

How desperate can someone sound? Esther thought, *she's known me less than an hour and she's blatantly trying to find out if I have a husband or not.*

"Oh, please, I've been gifted all of these things. I'm not one of those posh twats you see prancing about the place. As for the husband, you're barking up the wrong tree."

"Oh?" Gemma said, an expression of relief spreading across her face.

"What sort of woman do you take me for? You don't really think I'd be silly enough to be with a man, do you? Awful inventions... Women all the way," Esther said. She winked, hoping it would suffice.

And just like that, she had her. Like a moth to a flame. From then on, they'd been inseparable.

AFTER THE MURDER: THE INVESTIGATION

GEMMA

When Gemma was changed, she sent Esther a text telling her that she might be late home from work. She told her not to worry and that she was fine, but that there was a big case at work.

Although she felt guilty, she put her phone in her locker and turned it off. She couldn't afford to be distracted. She made her way into the conference room and braced herself for whatever there was to come.

"Good morning everyone. Hope you've got a coffee because this one's going to be a lot to take in. We've got a lot of work to do."

TOBY'S REVENGE

There was a moment of silence as the tension subsided and everyone adjusted themselves, shaking it off like rainwater from their coats.

"The victim is Emma Langley, better known by her students and their parents as Mrs Langley, English teacher from Le Petit Oak School over the road. Injuries are consistent with blunt head trauma, specifically the back of the skull, causing it to shatter. The object used is said to have been blunt, perhaps like a baseball bat or even a hammer. It was used with great force, indicating that the suspect will most likely be physically, very strong. We've run a background check on all men in the local area," Nigel said.

Gemma could sense the terror radiating from Nigel, seeping out of every pore. The red that previously stained both his cheeks subsided temporarily, substituted by a whitish grey.

TOBY'S REVENGE

There was only so much horror films could prepare you for. When you were in front of a dead body in real life, that's when you were introduced to what fear really was.

"What about her lips and her eyes? They look sort of sliced? Pretty precise. Nothing like a hammer," Gemma said as she rotated the image, failing miserably to stifle the retching sound that jumped in her throat like a trapped frog.

"Autopsy determines that her lips were cut off with a pair of classroom scissors kept in the draw for the students to use. The bastard took her eyelids off with them too. Sliced them right to the eyelashes."

"What about that? On her neck? What is that? Like some sort of rope or something?" one of the other colleagues asked.

"Unfortunately, no. That would be her large intestine. The killer sliced her open, pulled out her intestine and wrapped it around her neck. We're trying to work out whether this is some kind of personal thing or whether he's just a sadistic bastard," Nigel said, his emotional investment bleeding through.

Gemma swallowed hard. Her stomach flipped over and over.

Glances were exchanged between the team. Gemma had only seen these kinds of glances twice before. They were only really exchanged when the team was dealing with the most gruesome of cases. It was an expression of utter helplessness and fear. It was an expression that screamed, 'I know we're here to protect, but who will protect us?'

"What leads have we got?" Gemma asked, trying to shift the oppressive tone in the room.

Nobody said a word.

"Well, what are we waiting for? Let's get the bastard," Gemma demanded, incredulous.

"Forensics are all over it. We're waiting for a response from the lab. Then we can crack down on the interviews," Nigel said.

"And the family? What about her husband?"

"No siblings and her Mother and Father died three years ago in a car accident. We've been in contact with Mr. Langley. He's naturally in shock, but eager to cooperate and provide any information. We'll be as sensitive as possible; however, Mr. Langley, will of course, be considered a suspect."

"Thank you, Nigel. Right, everyone, do what you can. Draw up some files of potential suspects in the area. Maybe do a background check on all the school cleaners, see if they're physically well built. We can't leave any stone unturned. Gem, you're with me. See you all in an hour," Mick ordered.

Gemma got up and followed Mick into his office.

"You're off to the school today, Gem. We need to get some answers. You'll be interviewing some of the kids, asking them about anything they may have thought to be suspicious about their teacher, perhaps any conflicts she had with colleagues, anything."

Gemma nodded.

Mick's eyes fell to a black and white image framed on his cabinet. It presented a row of old houses and a large group of men, women and children congregated at what looked like a carnival stall. Underneath, a plaque read: **SUMMER CARNIVAL, OAKLEY GREEN, 1950**. Briefly, a look of pure joy presented itself on his face. Just as quickly as it had appeared, it was swiped off by the thought of Mrs Langley's murder. He wondered how on earth this town had become so dangerous. A town where people had always left their doors open, along with their hearts.

Gemma looked at the image and then back at Mick.

"We're going to get the bastard, Mick. I promise."

"Oh, Gem. I really hope so. I just hope to God it's not one of our own."

"Oh, it won't be, Mick. I've grown up with the people of this town. Hearts full of gold, the lot of them," Gemma affirmed, though her smile faltered slightly as she felt the doubt in her statement.

He gave a short nod and forced a smile.

Gemma got up to leave, turning the knob of the door.

"Oh, and Gem? remember, they're just kids."

BEFORE THE MURDER

EMMA

She felt like she was making a mistake when she and David moved to Oakley Green. She knew David was following his dream, starting his perfect career as a salesman. Would she have been considered an unsupportive wife is she hadn't gone with him? *Probably.*

It was too late, anyway. They'd already made a deposit on that great big house on the hill. It was an ugly thing, Emma thought, but David had obviously fallen completely in love with it and so, she couldn't have told him no.

Emma was extremely attractive, and to some extent, she was aware of it. She knew how to use her looks to get what she wanted. But with David, it never seemed that easy. It was like he saw through her looks, her charm. He saw through the irresistible golden bronzed skin, the glittering highlight that smothered her cheekbones, the blood orange lipstick that was packed on, layer after layer, concealing and suffocating the silicone filled lips beneath.

He gave the impression that he would never feel inferior to her, unlike so many other men. He was sure of himself, and perhaps Emma wasn't. But Emma was sure of what she wanted, and it wasn't David anymore. She was missing that electrifying sensation of being in love, that connection people rave on and on about.

She yearned for David's affection, for him to be overwhelmed as she stepped down the stairs modelling a little black dress before they made their way out to dinner.

"Darling, you look beautiful. I feel like the luckiest man in the room," He'd used to say. It made her feel so special. But, those years, it seemed were fading. It had all been substituted for constant nagging, kisses on the cheek and microwave meals.

The last time she had felt truly appreciated, truly in love was when she dated Esther Quinn, a girl she'd met in Paris. Esther had been on a gap year, but after meeting Emma, she wanted to stay a little longer because of her adoration for the city that grew daily. Emma didn't mind. She loved having Esther around.

It was like she had this magnetic pull, this trance that she could put you in instantly when you were in her presence. She would have followed Esther anywhere. But it wasn't the life she'd planned. She had told her parents she would marry a man and deep down she wanted to marry a man. She wanted children and a dog, all the conventional idealistic things that are promised once you were married. They both parted ways, but always kept the memory of each other in their hearts. Or at least, Emma did.

TOBY'S REVENGE

But, once she had the house, the husband, the dog, it all seemed strangely underwhelming. The glamour of it had worn off. She craved that feeling again. She began to think of Esther.

BEFORE THE MURDER

TOBY

Toby had always despised the people who lived in Oakley Green. He'd always agreed with his Father's opinion of them as advocates for idleness, living their conventional lives, discussions consisting of whether to repaint the kitchen or the living room. They never experienced any fun. They weren't cultured and they had no desire to be.

Toby's father was a great man. A real man. He'd always protected his family, upheld his reputation. After his death, Toby had lost all perspective of what was real. He had lost his sense of direction. His father was the only person he could trust.

His mother wasn't interested in the reputation the Devourt family had maintained for generations. Instead, she spent her time getting pissed, chain-smoking until all hours, blasting out droning songs on that ancient CD player of hers that she'd snagged at a tacky car boot sale the town sometimes put on to 'raise money for charity', *the charity of their own pockets more like.* She never loved Toby's father. She was with him for convenience. To say she had a husband.

He wanted to be great. He wanted to follow in his father's footsteps and be a legend in the town. He wanted the people of this town to speak about him for generations to come. He would be a beacon of hope, like those he idolised had been for him. Ted Bundy, John Wayne Gacy, Charles Manson. All the greats. He'd have that power and they would listen to him.

But he needed someone to notice his brilliance. He needed someone with a meticulous eye to help him, someone who shared the same goal.

TOBY'S REVENGE

As far as friends, Toby had never made many. He'd always been something of an outsider, a loner, some might say. He didn't mind that too much, however, sometimes he'd become lonely and think of his father, the only company he really wanted around. He didn't look like the other kids at school. He cared about his appearance.

He made an effort to comb his hair and ensure that his uniform had been washed and ironed every night. The others always appeared to be so juvenile. They'd forget to comb their hair, brush their teeth, iron their clothes. They lacked respect. It frustrated Toby, got under his skin.

Of course, he'd grown up in Oakley Green. He had never known another home. He was born in the house he still lived in. He'd always attended the local schools and town events. But for some reason, he just couldn't make any friends that would stick around.

AFTER THE MURDER: THE INVESTIGATION

MEETING TOBY

Gemma was parked in the school parking area. She sat there for a few minutes to gather herself. Flashbacks of torn, sliced flesh left and returned to her mind with gunshot velocity.

Upon entering the school, Gemma was greeted by a woman who skipped over to her like a dog who had caught sight of a bone. She held out her hand and introduced herself as Miss Skitter.

"Detective Gemma McCarthy. My deepest condolences for your loss," Gemma said with an insouciance that had become standard procedure. She couldn't help it. The job required someone thick skinned and almost devoid of all emotion. Gemma knew all too well that she was both of those things.

It looked like the walls had been bombarded by a Crayola set. There was so much colour, yet so much darkness to be felt when walking the halls. There were inspiring quotes thrown about sporadically. One of which, read 'live the life you love. Love the life you live.'

Well, I suppose we can try, Gemma thought.

Then there was a smell. Gemma had smelt it many times, but never in a school. She began rubbing her arms to supress the goose bumps that formed. The thought of Mrs Langley's corpse lying cold and still on the floor of her classroom for what could have been hours. The classroom she would have once paced passionately around, helping to inspire the next generation of Oakley Green. Heat rose within her. This burning anger, it consumed her. It was in her blood now. She had to catch the man who did this.

"Now, as I say the students are really just d-d-delicate f-f-flowers. Their petals have really been just ripped out you see, bless the little loves! Well we all have been q-quite upset really, I mean s-s-she was a nice woman, do you know what I mean? Oh! I didn't offer you a tea or coffee. Do you like sug-

"

"Miss Skitter," Gemma interjected. She placed a hand on her shoulder to comfort her, "I appreciate the introduction, really. I understand this is a very confusing time for you and the students. I'd just like to get this over and done with so that we do the best we can regarding solving the case and begin the healing process. I'm sure you feel the same."

Miss Skitter went stiff. Her lower lip began to tremble. Gemma noticed tears forming in her eyes.

"I j-just don't understand. Funny thing isn't it? Death."

Gemma waited for a few seconds before asking about Mrs Langley whilst Miss Skitter sobbed and sniffled. Gemma handed her a tissue which she accepted desperately.

"When was the last time you saw Mrs Langley, Miss Skitter?"

"I was in work on the T-T-Tuesday. I was taking over her class because she h-had to be at an appointment. She left early after the break time, only, she didn't tell me where or what it was about. I mean, I know that it was none of my business, but we'd become a little c-c-closer than usual and I'd always assured her that she could tell me anything."

"Did you notice anything suspicious about her actions that day? Was she on edge or acting out of the ordinary?"

"She w-wasn't like that. She was a-always happy. I guess, she was a little chirpier that day b-but even then, I can't tell if that's just me overthinking."

Gemma watched as Miss Skitter fiddled with her hands. She began darting her eyes left to right.

"Well if you think of anything, it's important to let us know... anything."

Miss Skitter didn't answer. Instead, she wiped her eyes, nodded compliantly and led Gemma to the meeting room where the interviews would be taking place.

"Well, I'll b-be going now. Tea and c-c-coffee are over in the corner," Miss Skitter said, turning on her heel, eager to leave.

"Miss Skitter," Gemma called, not turning around to face her, "a secret is no longer a secret when the person you're keeping it for is dead. Believe me," Gemma said.

Miss Skitter opened her mouth to speak but instead, scurried off.

Gemma sat down at the table which had a register on it. It listed all the students who were taught by Mrs Langley. There were only twenty students in her class, and another class of twenty-five she'd covered. Just as she was skimming over the list, Gemma was interrupted by the piercing sound of the bell.

"Bloody hell," she muttered, jumping, "bring them in."

After the first lot of interviews, Gemma wondered whether it was all a waste of time. The kids weren't saying anything out of the ordinary, like she was pretty and kind and was always fair with marking. Most of them had placed bouquets of flowers outside the classroom where the crime scene was still under investigation. Gemma wondered what Mrs Langley could have been hiding or what she could have done for someone to replace all those roses with a deadly thorn.

Gemma looked at her watch. 1.pm. and nothing to report back. There was one name she hadn't crossed off yet. A young boy named Toby Devourt. He was the last interview for the day.

At that point, Gemma was startled by a firm knock on the door. As she bent down to pick up her pen that had rolled off the table, she noticed the shoes of this young boy. Oddly pristine, she thought for a young boy of fourteen. She'd been expecting them to be covered with dirt from messing around on the field at break time like so many young boys did.

"Hello there. You must be Toby?" Gemma asked, grinning in that way all adults deem to be the correct way of greeting children and teenagers.

She pulled a chair out and gestured for him to take a seat.

He wasn't receptive to this approach. Instead, he remained silent. He stood in the doorway analysing Gemma for a few seconds, coercing her to look down at herself. As he sauntered over to the seat, he took out a bottle of hand sanitiser. He rubbed his hands in circular motions, placed the lid back on the bottle and then held his hand out for Gemma to shake.

"Eh, I haven't got the lurgies," Gemma joked.

He didn't laugh or smile at this either. He sat there, face straight and serious, his arms crossed tightly.

Gemma coughed awkwardly and then sat, shuffling her papers. This was the first time she'd ever felt intimidated by a younger person. It was like he had this intangible force over her. He made her feel anxious, like she had to be better than she was, like she had to reach his level before he would even consider speaking to her.

"So, Toby. My name is – "

"Detective McCarthy," Toby interrupted, "You're here to catch who killed Mrs Langley."

"That's ... correct, Toby. Now, I'm here because your teacher, Mrs Langley, she-" Gemma stopped. Her and kids weren't a compatible combination. She never knew how to talk to them.

"I know. She's dead," Toby said, "It's okay. You don't need to treat me like a baby. I know I look like a child, but I can assure you, I'm frightfully intelligent."

Gemma leant back in her seat and gazed at Toby.

"You know, you remind me of myself at your age. It's not easy. Adults being adults. Bet you feel like you're being kept in the dark, eh?"

"You're not supposed to do that, you know," Toby said, focusing his eyes on Gemma's chair legs, suspended in the air as she leant backwards.

"You're not going to tell on me, are you?" Gemma said, raising an eyebrow, trying her luck.

There was still no sign of a smile.

Toby shook his head, "I'm no snitch."

Gemma quickly began feeling like she wasn't speaking with a young boy at all, but a mob leader. It was the way he spoke; it was much more mature than all the others she'd spoken with that day. He had an air of wisdom for someone so young. It was like he had comprehended the complexities of the adult world with no trouble at all.

"Right... well, thank God for that then," Gemma said, unsure what to do with herself.

"Toby, tell me about your relationship with Mrs Langley. Did you think she was a good teacher?"

"She was my teacher. I didn't like her, I didn't dislike her," Toby said, shrugging.

"Did you feel like you could talk to her if you needed to?"

"Teachers don't really like me," Toby said, bowing his head.

Gemma leant forward, "Hey, don't say that. Look, I know teachers can be a little bit mardy sometimes, but it's because they want to help you learn. They're here to keep you safe."

"Teach me a lesson, you mean," Toby said with a thickness in his voice. His eyebrows grew closer together, pointing downwards. Under the table, Gemma could feel him kicking his legs. An almost burgundy shade emerged on his cheeks.

Gemma began to feel uncomfortable. She sensed Toby's rage, bubbling on the edge of eruption. It resonated with her.

"Hey, Toby. Listen," Gemma said, she slid her hand nearer to Toby's, "if you need to talk to someone about something, I'm sure there are teachers here who would listen."

"They hate me. They think I'm different. I hear them talking about me and gossiping," Toby said. He kicked his feet harder under the table.

"Now, that just can't be true. The teachers here care about each one of you. I know it's been difficult since Mrs Lang- "

"Especially her. She's the one who started it!" Toby blurted violently, screwing his hand up into a fist, the skin stretched white over his small knuckles.

"Woah, woah, Toby. What do you mean? Who started what?" Gemma panicked, backing away.

Toby's jaw clenched along with everything else that could be, "I'm leaving now," he demanded.

"Toby. Listen, I know that what happened to Mrs Langley has been rea- "

"Just stop saying that. She's dead. Why do people only care when you're dead?" Toby gabbled, "When you're dead, you're gone. And she is. She's dead."

Gemma sat back, speechless. Before she had time to ask Toby anymore questions, the sound of Miss Skitter's heels clip-clopping against the laminate flooring broke their gaze.

"Toby, your time is up. P-Please, j-j-join the others in assembly."

Toby darted a look at Gemma. In his eyes, Gemma saw pain and a story, a story she felt they might share.

"Toby," Gemma called after him. She was too late. He'd been led away. What did he mean she'd started it? Was Mrs Langley really the innocent English teacher she appeared to be, or was there something she was hiding? Something terrible?

Gemma flew around the corner into the parking bay outside the Station. She turned with such speed that her tyres left marks on the tarmac.

When she'd stormed her way through the front door, she made her way immediately to Mick's office to report back. When she got to the door, she didn't knock like she usually did, but she figured Mick would dismiss this due to the urgency of the case. She pushed the door open and hovered for a minute.

There he was. There she was. Mick. Linda. The pair were rubbing up against each other. On his neck and face, bright red lipstick was smeared. Upon seeing Gemma, the pair split hastily.

Gemma stood, her mouth gaped open, her eyes narrowed, "Oh, I should have known," she said, "looks like some *really* important police work you're doing here."

TOBY'S REVENGE

"Gem," Mick started, but was hastily cut off by Gemma's slamming of his office door.

Gemma stormed to her car and opened the door. She nearly yanked the door off its hinges, jumped in and slammed it shut. She grabbed the aux cable connected to the cd player, plugged her phone in and blasted out the *OK Computer* album by Radiohead.

Inside, Esther was making dinner. When Gemma pushed her way through the front door and into the hallway, the delicious scent of herbs and spices greeted her, making her feel warm and content.

"Fuck my life," Gemma called, chucking down her bag and kicking her shoes off.

"Babe? What's up?" Esther asked, peeking round the kitchen door, sporting a red and white polka dot apron, sweat forming on her brow and gravy smeared all over the backs of her hands.

"Oh, nothing out of the ordinary, just fucking work."

TOBY'S REVENGE

As if it was a routine, Esther made her way to the cupboard and reached for a wine glass. She then skipped to the fridge and poured a large glass of Merlot. She then grabbed a coaster and set it down next to Gemma, delicately positioning the wine down like it was worth millions.

"Only one glass though babe, remember? You've done really well this year," Esther said, smiling and rubbing Gemma's back.

"Mm, yes," Gemma uttered, taking a well-deserved gulp.

"Go on then, what's happened?" Esther asked again.

"Oh babe, it's nothing. I just have this awful case. School teacher, early thirties, intelligent, attractive, had the rest of her career ahead of her. She's been brutally tortured and killed in her own classroom. You couldn't write it," Gemma said, taking another big gulp.

"Oh, wow. You must be beside yourself," Esther said, putting her arm around Gemma, "Was there much blood?"

Gemma was silent for a minute, looking away. Then, turning to Esther, she took a long and deep breath, "babe, it was like nothing I've ever seen before."

"Did she suffer?" Esther asked, this time, eyes wild and ready to drink in all the detail.

"She must have. The bastard cut her eyelids off and her lips with a pair of the classroom scissors of all things! Honestly, babe it was horrendous, but nothing I can't handle," Gemma assured Esther, reaching for her hand and stroking it.

"And her wedding ring, was it still on her hand?" Esther asked as she made her way over to check on the dinner, her back to Gemma.

As Gemma went to answer, she hesitated. Her face twisted slightly as she realised that she'd never told Esther about whether Emma Langley was married or not. Why would she ask? The question lingered in Gemma's mind, and just as she was about to confront Esther about it, she was interrupted by the banging and scratching around of plates and cutlery.

"Dinner's ready babe and I made your favourite. Roast Chicken."

Gemma smiled, shrugging Esther's question off and putting it to the back of her mind as a mere coincidence.

"You would tell me, wouldn't you? If you needed time off work. I can put in extra hours at the college. They really wouldn't mind," Esther insisted.

Extra hours at the college? Gemma thought, *you barely do full time hours, it's hardly extra.* She'd volunteered at first, then a few months afterwards a position came up for an Assistant Administrator. Being unemployed, Esther took it immediately, but Gemma knew it was her income that contributed the most to their rent and bills. She didn't have the heart to ask Esther to do more, she felt almost guilty at the thought.

"I'll be alright. I've got you, haven't I," Gemma said, kissing Esther on the cheek as she came and sat beside her.

"Always," Esther said, grinning, "You'll never get rid of me, no matter how hard you try."

The following morning, Gemma made her way to the Station. She went straight into Mick's office. It was something about Toby that didn't sit right with her. She had this feeling, deep in the pit of her stomach.

"I wanted to tell you something. It's about one of the kids from the school, Mick."

"Who?" Mick asked as he scoffed the last of a packet of scotch eggs.

"A lad called Toby Devourt."

Mick's face changed. There was a graveness to it, like something had returned, something that had been haunting him.

"Ah, Greg's son. Quite a handful, so I've heard."

"Eh? Who's Greg? You know what, this town might not be so small after all. Thought I knew everyone."

Mick's fist clenched slightly. He looked back at the old photograph of Oakley Green, then back at Gemma.

"Years ago, the Devourts and the Porters had a bit of, what you could call a dispute over who acquired which part of land in the town. My Grandfather, Matthew Porter had made it clear he and his family were going to be running a farm on the part of land that the Devourts were planning on acquiring. Let's just say they didn't take it too well. Ever since, there's been friction."

"Sounds like some kind of medieval tale," Gemma said, smirking, "anyway, what's that got to do with Toby?"

"Well, I'm not one to assume, Gem, but his father, Greg, died last year. He was what you'd call your typical hard man. He'd done some quite unpleasant things in his time, some of which I won't mention. Didn't like me, that's for sure. Had him in a few times for GBH. He'd also had a track record for burglary. I just wonder, naturally, if the apple doesn't fall far from the tree. What did you think of him?"

"Well, he certainly wasn't cooperative, Jesus Christ. If he were mine, he'd be getting a right good telling off."

"So, what was it about him?" Mick asked, eyes glistening with intrigue.

"I asked him about Mrs Langley, as I did with all the other children. But, this time, it was different. His entire attitude changed. He went off on one when I mentioned Mrs Langley. It was like he couldn't stand her. Whatever was inside, he's been trying to keep it in."

"Mm, that is strange. Did he say anything about their relationship? Did they get along?"

"Well, actually that's what I wanted to talk about with you. He told me that she had started something? Although, I couldn't quite make out what he meant."

"Mm, keep your notes to reference back to. Maybe you could speak with him again when you interview the teachers? Just to see if he gives you anything else to report back. We need to be looking out for these things, every detail counts."

"Yeah, of course. I'll be on my way then," Gemma said, passing her notes over and making her way out.

***

Back at the Le Petit Oak, Gemma parked in the same place. She felt nervous this time, but excited, like she might be getting somewhere with the case.

"Detective, y-y-you're back again, any p-p-progression with the case?" Miss Skitter greeted Gemma at the reception.

"Miss Skitter, hi, I'm afraid I'll need to speak to one of your students again. Toby Devourt, please."

Miss Skitter's body shivered slightly. Her smile faded, "C-certainly. I'll go and fetch him now. H-he's n-n-not in any trouble, is he?"

"Oh, no. Just a follow up from our conversation. We didn't quite get to finish our chat and there were a few more questions I wanted to ask him."

Miss Skitter sped off to find him, escorted him to reception and then left, not saying a word.

"Detective Gemma McCarthy," Toby said in a way a talk show host introduces a celebrity. He held out his hand for Gemma to shake. As she did, she felt the clammy moisture of the sanitising gel he'd used the time she first met him.

"Toby," Gemma said, pulling away from his grip after a few seconds, "I just wanted to know if you'd be up for answering some more questions regarding the case? Would that be alright?"

"Of course," He grinned knowingly, "poor Mrs Langley."

It was something about the way he'd said it that made Gemma's skin itch. There was a fraction of her that was deeply intimidated by him, although she couldn't quite put her finger on it.

They both sat in the room they'd been assigned to previously. It was a bland room. There were a few puzzles piled high in the corner by the window, creating a barrier between them and the natural light. The walls were a non-descript magnolia. Toby's hair was scraped back with an excessive amount of gel. Each hair had its own place, he'd used a comb, giving his parting more definition. It was so neat. He could have been on one of those cringe worthy children's adverts for George Asda looking all blonde, blue-eyed, perfect and put together.

"So, looks like we're here again then, eh," Gemma said, her voice echoing.

"It does, Detective."

"Look, Toby. I'm not going to beat around the bush here because this is serious, and you seem like an intelligent young man. I want to know what you meant from our previous conversation when you were talking about Mrs Langley starting it?"

"What would you like to know, Detective?"

"Well, let's start with the statement about Mrs Langley starting something, shall we?"

Toby looked up at the ceiling. He looked around as if this conversation was the most brain-numbing thing he'd ever embarked on.

"Well, I heard her and some other teachers talking about me and my family, about how I would probably end up like my deadbeat father if I didn't buck my ideas up. But they've no idea what it's like, the pressure of doing well and processing the death of my father simultaneously."

He was right. They probably didn't understand. A part of Gemma knew about the pressure that Toby was under. *At least Toby's father was dead*, Gemma thought. Perhaps her teenage years would have been different if she had been grieving a parent who was dead. Instead, she grieved her father who was very much alive, causing her mother harm, day in, day out. She grieved for who he was before.

"Well, I'm sorry that you had to hear that, Toby. My family was the talk of the Town too when I was around your age. People can be vicious, but you have to remember, they're only words."

Toby didn't respond. He explored Gemma's face with his pearlescent eyes, focusing specifically on her hair. She guessed he was thinking about how incongruous it was compared to all the other long silky styles the women of this town sported.

"You're in love with a woman, aren't you?" Toby asked, his face blank.

Gemma let out a small laugh, "You got that from just looking at my hair? Wow, you should take my job."

"Does she look like you too?"

Esther's face came up in Gemma's mind. Her mousy brown hair effortlessly draped across her feminine shoulders, her high cheekbones, deep green eyes that sparkled in the natural light like spheres of precious glass.

"No, nothing like me at all," Gemma said, smiling at the thought.

"The thing is, Detective, Mrs Langley was behaving awfully disrespectfully towards me during a conversation I overheard between herself and one of her colleagues," Toby said, his face bitter at the reminder.

"And, when you heard this conversation, what was it that you did?"

"Well, I did nothing of course, until I got home. I told my mother."

"And what did she say you should do?"

"She told me to take no notice, that the woman was probably unhappy with her own life and that we were always going to receive prejudices from town folk because of how my father had behaved in previous years."

Gemma thought back to what Mick had told her about Toby's father, Greg Devourt. Maybe he really did have an impact on the town. More so than Gemma thought.

"I'm sorry, Toby. I don't mean to bring up any memories of your father. I know what it's like to lose a parent and have people speak about them as though their lives were just gossip."

"I understand, really it's fine, Detective."

"Toby, please, call me Gemma."

This appeared to have annoyed Toby slightly. He seemed confused. Gemma couldn't quite figure out why, but it was like he had been offended by her openness.

"Gemma?"

"Yes, Toby?"

"I'm not sure that Mrs Langley was a good person."

"What makes you say that?"

"Well, it's just, the way she was murdered. She must have betrayed someone in the worst way, someone she knew.

That doesn't sound like a good person to me. Good people don't hurt the ones they love, do they?"

When Gemma got home, she traipsed in with mucky boots, slid them off and slumped herself up each stair. She sat there for a minute, zoning out. Then, she noticed Esther's shoes were missing from their usual place on the shoe rack.

"Esther?" she called up from the bottom of the stairs. There was no answer.

Then, the part of their room with the loose floorboard let out a faint creak, though, loud enough for Gemma to hear from the stairs.

Gemma's made her way upstairs to their room, suspicion growing with each step. There was no faint light spilling out from the gap underneath the bedroom door. There usually was when Esther was reading. She'd read and wait up for Gemma when she got in so they could catch up about the day they'd both had. *She's probably had a sulk and fallen asleep*, Gemma thought. But surely, she would have woken up and answered? Even so, that didn't explain why her shoes were missing.

Gemma's heart hammered against her chest. It was so loud it almost drowned out the sound of her fractured breathing. Once she'd reached the door, her breathing got faster and harder to control. Putting a shaking hand out against the door, Gemma pushed it open. It groaned open, freaking her out more than usual.

Gemma let out a quivering breath. Her lips trembled as she took a step forward. The darkness rendered it difficult for Gemma to read the situation. She could barely see anything. Her head jerked to the side and turned to see if she could see Esther sleeping. She wasn't there. The bed was neatly made.

Gemma felt beads of sweat form on her forehead. Someone had been there in her bedroom; she was sure of it.

She knew what she'd heard. She reached for her phone with her trembling hands, dialled Esther's number and waited for her to pick up. Standing there in the darkness alone, the ringing sounded louder than usual, only contributing to her paranoia.

As suspected, there was no answer. She pressed the hash key on her keyboard and left a voicemail.

"Esther. It's me. You're scaring the shit out of me. Where the hell are you? Call me when you get this."

Another hour had passed. Gemma couldn't stand it any longer. She'd already succeeded in biting all the skin off around her nails, enough to make them bleed. She was going out of her mind and Esther it seemed, didn't care. She thought maybe Esther was just acting out because of how busy Gemma had been at work. *Maybe she's turned her phone off and gone into town to find herself somebody who paid her all the attention she needed all the time*, Gemma thought, but then her stomach dropped at the thought of that happening.

After hours of imagining where Esther was or who she was with, Gemma decided to take a long hot bath to calm her nerves. *Two can play that game*, she thought, switching her phone off and chucking it on the bed. *She'll be back, apologetically pissed or something.*

Whilst in the bath, Gemma thought about her conversation with Toby. She wondered what he had meant about Mrs Langley starting something. She didn't really get much out of him, not as much as she'd wanted anyway. But then she supposed, people shouldn't be rushed into opening up to you about things. They took their own time. Maybe she'd have to practice patience and simply wait for the revelation this case needed.

Toby had reminded her of the times she felt shut out during her parents' divorce. It was the way he looked as though he was harnessing so much pain. She knew more than anyone what that felt like.

After her parents' divorce, she went downhill. Drinking all day, every day. Unemployed. Getting into fights. If it wasn't for the opportunity to become a Detective, Gemma didn't know what would have happened. Then, she thought of Esther. She thought about how much Esther had changed her life. She'd finally found a woman who loved her for her, flaws and all. A sudden feeling of guilt washed over her. Maybe she had been too distant with Esther. Maybe she'd allowed work to take over her life.

Once she'd got out for the bath and put her pyjamas on, Gemma decided that now was long enough for Esther to not be returning her calls. It was inexcusable and as her fiancé, she should keep her updated out of respect. It was odd for Esther to do this; she'd never just impulsively take off like that.

"Come on, pick up, old git," Gemma moaned, dialling Mick's number.

"Bloody hell Gem, what time do you call this?"

"Look, Mick, there's no time to piss about here. It's Esther. She hasn't been home for hours and I don't even know how long she's been gone for but she's not returning my calls."

There was a long silence, followed by a sigh.

"Does she know about...?"

"Yes, she knows about the case. Not everything, but I've told her enough."

"Oh God. Have you tried phoning her?" Mick said.

"No, I've just left it for hours in the hope she comes back. Of course, I've bloody called her," Gemma spat.

"No need to be sarcastic Gem. I'm just trying to help. Look, if she doesn't call back in the next hour, I'll request a search party," Mick said. There was an unease in his voice which made Gemma's stomach turn.

"Mick, what if something terrible has happened to her? she's all I've got, Mick. She's all I've got."

It was morning. Esther hadn't responded to any of Gemma's calls. Gemma's eyes were red-rimmed, her head thick. She'd hardly slept at all. She sat herself up in bed, flicking through photographs of her and Esther on her phone. The tears started again, pricking her eyes. She was so sorry. She was sorry about being so consumed by work and missing the adoption meeting. She was sorry that she didn't pay Esther enough attention. She was just so sorry.

Gemma rolled out of bed and made her way downstairs, stopping suddenly to look at the carpet. *Esther chose that carpet*, a little voice in her head whispered to her. They'd had a row about it for weeks but as usual, she got her own way.

She'd always had her own way, with everything. Gemma couldn't help it. Esther had stolen her heart and Gemma had no intention of asking for it back.

As she was making coffee, Gemma's phone buzzed. She jumped at the thought of Esther responding. This feeling then died when she saw a text from Mick asking if she'd had any luck with Esther. She replied, letting him know that she wasn't coming in until Esther had come back. He'd told her that was fine, but she doubted it. This case was a priority and they needed the entire team on it. But at that moment, Esther was her priority. She was her own little investigation.

When she made her coffee, Gemma sat on the kitchen table, just thinking. Racking her brains about where Esther could have gone and about why. It dawned on her that she might have gone to stay with her mum. She'd often taken off and told Gemma she was going back to spend some time with her family for a weekend or two. It never bothered Gemma, she understood, but this time, it seemed odd. Why wouldn't she let her know?

Gemma riffled through the list of numbers that Esther left on the side. *Ah-ha.* She rang and rang but there was no answer. Esther's mother never liked Gemma from the start. She was a bad influence on their precious princess. Homosexuality was a phase, apparently. Seven years later and they were still adamant.

Eventually, Esther's mum picked up.

"Esther, love?"

"Oh, actually, Joan it's me, Gem. I didn't know if you'd saved my number?"

There was an awkward silence.

"Is Esther okay?"

Gemma swallowed hard, attempting to hold her tears back, "Well, actually I was going to- "

The jangling of keys in the door caused Gemma to throw the phone down. In the doorway, soaking wet was Esther. She looked like she'd seen a ghost.

"Esther," Gemma started, tearing up, "I've been worried sick. I thought..."

Esther looked at Gemma with guilt in her eyes, "I'm really sorry. I just needed to... I just n-need to..."

Before she could finish, Esther collapsed like a dishevelled garden chair onto the ground in tears, howling.

"Esther! Tell me what's happened please you're scaring me," Gemma pleaded, holding Esther tight and kissing her profusely on her forehead.

Esther was inconsolable, only managing small fragments of a conversation through sporadic fits of crying.

Gemma knew she wouldn't get anywhere with Esther like that. She'd wait until morning when Esther's head was clear. When she'd had rest and time to think things through.

TOBY'S REVENGE

After putting Esther to bed, Gemma made her way downstairs, stared at a bottle of Merlot next to the fridge. She darted her eyes towards a wine glass and then stopped. She drew in a deep breath and shook her head. She could have done with a drink. She *really* could have done with it, but Esther meant more, and so did her career. *Stop it, what's wrong with you?* She hissed to herself. She'd made significant progress with giving up the alcohol. She couldn't start again just because things got tough.

Considering she couldn't sleep, Gemma decided to make herself a cup of tea, get her laptop out and start looking into Mrs Langley some more. Once she'd opened Google Chrome, she was in. The Great British Stalk off began. She was always brilliant at that. Friends would gossip about who they were going on a blind date with, oblivious about where they were from, who they were friends with and what they did for a job. That's when Gemma stepped in. She'd find out in minutes all the information they'd ever need to know. It was in her blood, to chase, to dissect, to discover.

She was surprised that she'd never spoken to Mrs Langley, or bumped into her before, given the size of Oakley Green. The town was tiny in comparison to most.

She typed **Mrs Emma Langley, Oakley Green** into Google. As expected, a range of different images and irrelevant profiles of different people came up. Gemma scrolled her way through endless pages of fabricated bullshit. Then, just when she thought all hope was lost, she stumbled across a Facebook profile. It confirmed her full name:

Emma Langley, Occupation: English Teacher at *Le Petit Oak*, Oakley Green. Relationship Status: Married.

An image of her alive, revealed just how beautiful she really was. Bright green eyes with a hint of hazel, complimented by olive skin and long dark brown hair. *No wonder she had enemies*, Gemma thought. The woman was an absolute Goddess.

As she scrolled down on her profile, Gemma noticed messages left by her students and colleagues, none of which looked suspicious. All of them expressing their admiration for her and what a wonderful person she'd been. Then, Gemma waded through every individual photo. There was no photographic evidence of her and her Husband. It struck Gemma as strange. Surely, you'd want to show your partner off?

The images consisted largely of her, her friends and family on holidays. Cinematic images, almost like they were photoshopped they were that seamless. Bright skies, white sandy beaches, slim, toned bodies and videos showing the clinking together of glasses.

Becoming lost in Emma Langley's perfect life, Gemma lost track of the time. It was getting late. *I better get to bed,* she thought, closing all the tabs on her desktop. Then, just as she was closing down each tab, she noticed an image on Emma Langley's Facebook that she must have scrolled past and missed before.

At first, she couldn't believe her eyes. She froze. It couldn't be.

She zoomed in and out and in and out again and again until she was satisfied. Mousy brown hair, beautiful eyes, feminine shoulders. Low and behold, stood with her arms draped round Emma Langley's neck. Posing in Paris, showered with sunshine. Esther.

Gemma jumped up like a flash and pushed her laptop across the table until it almost fell off the edge. *No fucking way.*

When Gemma had opened the curtains to let the morning sun in, Esther was still fast asleep, snoring her head off. Gemma stood over her and wondered who her Fiancé really was. At that moment, Gemma visualised herself pouring her hot coffee over Esther's head. She watched as her darling fiancé tossed and turned like a baby, blissfully unaware of what she'd put Gemma through. Eventually, when she woke, her body convulsed in shock at the sight of Gemma.

"Shit, babe. You startled me."

"Oh, Sorry."

Esther stroked Gemma's hand, "It's okay babe. I should be sorry, about last night."

Gemma shook her hand away, "where were you? Last night?"

"I had some bad news about an old friend I used to know. She died. I just wanted to get out."

"Oh, I'm so sorry," Gemma said through gritted teeth. Her face was stiff, and her skin felt tight.

Esther smiled. She wiped away imaginary tears and carried as if nothing had happened. She continued to pretend that she hadn't had Gemma waiting up all night wondering where the hell her fiancé was. What else, Gemma wondered, was Esther pretending not to know.

"What was her name? did I know her?"

"Look, babe, do you mind if we don't talk about it. It's still pretty raw."

Gemma's heart sank. Could it really be true? Esther had been lying to her about knowing Emma Langley?

"Well, actually, I do mind," Gemma insisted.

Esther sniggered, "excuse me?"

"I'm going to ask you something, and I want you to tell me the truth because that's what I deserve."

Esther's face screwed up. She became restless.

"Gem, what is this?"

"How the *fuck* do you know Emma Langley?"

Esther became a statue of herself.

"Well?"

"I don't- "

"I swear to God, if you lie to me, we're over. I have evidence, Esther. Photographs of you two together in Paris."

Esther raised her arms, just like there were actual guns pointed at her.

"Woah, calm down, Gem. Please, you're scaring me."

"Don't tell me what to do. Now tell me how you know the victim of the case I'm working on and why the fuck you didn't think it a good idea to tell me this information."

Esther sighed, "you wouldn't believe me."

"Oh, try me. I've got all day."

"I met her before I met you. We met in Paris, during my gap year."

"Why didn't I ever meet her? She lived here. Did you come here together?"

"No, no. Gem. I did it to protect you."

"Protect me from what?"

Esther bowed her head.

"Oh my God. You and her. You were together? Like that? So, she wasn't just a friend?"

Esther didn't make a sound. Instead, she just sat there, fidgeting with her hands and hoping this mess would clear itself up.

Gemma could almost taste the bile from her stomach that made its way up to the back of her throat.

"You've been cheating on me?"

"Gem, no. Please don't think that. I know it looks bad- "

"Oh, it looks bloody terrible. Absolutely fucked up is what it looks like."

"I didn't know she was here until a few months ago. I was doing the food shopping. I bumped into her down the Vegetable and Fruit aisle. Her trolley knocked into mine and I was about to give her an earful, but then, I realised, it was Em."

Gemma's blood boiled at Esther's abbreviation of Emma's name. It was sickening. She could imagine it now, the pair of them fondling, calling each other nicknames they'd created. Sharing private jokes for all the little private things they knew about each other. About each other's bodies. All their little foibles that no one would ever be worthy of discovering. The jealousy was uncontrollable and multiplying by the second.

"We recognised each other instantly. I mean, it had been a few years, but I would recognise her face anywhere," Esther stopped, looked away and sighed deeply, "She was my first love."

Gemma felt physical pain. It was like someone had stabbed her. She couldn't bear to hear Esther speak so affectionately about another woman. But if this case was going to get solved, it was necessary to hear everything. She had to power on and shut her emotions out.

"And what did you say when you saw her?"

"Well, I was obviously shocked. I mean, from what I knew, Em was planning to stay in Paris for life. She had always talked about wanting to settle down there, maybe have kids and a little house on the outskirts. I had no idea she moved here. Honestly, I didn't. Once the shock wore off, we hugged, and I asked her what on earth she was doing here."

"And, what was her story? Why was she here?"

"She explained that she had married in Paris, just as she had planned. She was married to a man, which surprised me, but whatever, she seemed happy. She said her husband got offered his dream job in England, and so, she came with him. She seemed supportive, I thought it was sweet. They weren't going to move to Oakley Green at first, they were considering Birmingham apparently, but his family was closer to this end."

"Sounds touching. Did you have any contact after that?"

"Jesus, Gem. I feel like one of the convicts you bring in."

"Just answer the question," Gemma snapped.

Esther let out a sigh, burying her head in her hands.

"I told her that I was engaged, to a wonderful woman. A strong woman. She was happy for me. I told her I was happy for her too and that I might see her around. She smiled, walked away and then I went home."

"How can I believe you? What's to say you didn't come back with her here and finish what you'd started back in Paris?"

"My word, Gem. You have my word. I love you. I am marrying you."

"Why lie?"

"Gem, I didn't want to lose you over something that happened years ago. I've changed since then, that was my past. I didn't want you thinking anything of it."

"So, when I came home from work the other day and told you about the case, you didn't have any suspicions that it was her? She didn't tell you what she did for work? It didn't cross your mind for a second that who I was describing might be Emma?"

"As I said, it was a short chat, I was shocked. It never crossed my mind to ask. I got a call from her husband. Em had apparently written about me in a diary she kept years ago. She'd always kept one. My number was still in her contacts on her phone with my picture. He asked me if I knew who would have wanted to hurt Emma? Who would have wanted to kill her like that? Once he'd gone into more detail about the ordeal, it all began making sense."

"So, you thought you'd run away, instead of confiding in me?"

"I didn't tell you straight away. I wanted to deal with it myself first, so I went out and got some air. You would have been angry. I hadn't even intended to see her again so I suppose that's why I never told you. But I should have, I see that now. It hasn't been easy, processing this. Besides, I know how much stress you've been under with work and I didn't want to fuel the fire."

Gemma laughed, "Don't blame this on me. You've lied to me. You've kept valuable information from me. This could mess up my whole career, you know, the career I've always wanted?"

"I know, and I'm sorry but if you were easier to talk to these days, then maybe I would have let you in."

Gemma froze. She stared at Esther with pure hatred, grabbed her coat and made her way towards the door.

"How dare you!" She bellowed.

"Gemma, I'm sorry. I shouldn't have said that, where are you going?"

"To do my job," Gemma said, slamming the door behind her.

BEFORE THE MURDER

EMMA

David was being a dick. He'd been making digs at her all day. The fridge was empty. The house was an absolute mess, but *of course*, that was her problem.

"I'm going to the shop, Dave. Any requests before I leave?" Emma asked nicely.

He grunted. Then, nothing.

When Emma parks up outside the shop, she stops for a minute, takes a deep breath and prepares herself for small talk with parents at the school. Just because she's a teacher didn't mean people had the right to constantly bombard her with questions during her time off. But still, they did, and still, she complied, informed the parents of how precious their little darlings were, always reverting to that thought niggling at her that one day she and David would probably have to conceive. She didn't think she was completely ready to do that. Not with him, at least.

This time around, when she passed the Fruit and Vegetable aisle, Emma froze. Right there, in front, pushing her trolley full to the brim with nutritious goods. Long mousy brown hair and two emeralds for eyes. Esther.

She waited until Esther had spotted her too. There was no way she would have approached her first. The embarrassment would be far too much to cope with.

At that moment, her legs turned into jelly. She started playing with her hair, twisting it around her index finger self-consciously. *Did she look sexy? Would Esther think she'd dodged a bullet? Was Esther still into women? Or had they just been a phase she'd rather just forget*

BEFORE THE MURDER

ESTHER

She'd only popped into the supermarket for a couple of things for dinner that night. Spices, herbs, little insignificant things really. She never expected in a million years to be smacked in the face by her past. Could it have been? Emma. Em. *Her* Emma. The love of her life. She was here! In Oakley Green, of all places. But, why? How?

Mustering up every inch of courage she had, Esther took a deep breath, gave Emma a crooked smile and staggered forward. All of a sudden, she'd forgotten how to walk.

"Esther," Emma said, her voice almost breaking.

Esther smiled for a few seconds longer than she intended.

"Oh, Em. How- "

"How have you been?" Emma interrupted.

The cheap yellow lighting of the supermarket exposed the beads of sweat that were bursting on Emma's forehead. Esther pretended not to notice, but now and again, her eyes would slip up and fixate on it, causing Emma to keep wiping her head.

"Wow, what brings you to Oakley Green? I, I thought you were staying in Paris?"

Emma flushed red. The mentioning of Paris, perhaps, triggering her.

"Well, it's Dave, my husband. He got offered a job here as a Sales Manager. It was his dream job and so, we moved here. We were going to move to Birmingham, but Dave's family are nearer here," Emma said, wetting her lips every other second.

"Oh, wow. A *husband*. It seems like you got everything you ever wanted, doesn't it?" Esther said, genuinely happy for her, though, there was a slight slither of jealousy.

"Yeah, I suppose. And what about yourself? Married?"

"Engaged, actually."

Emma fell back slightly as if this news had shot right through her.

"Wow, Esther. That's great. I'm really happy for you. What's his name?"

"Her, actually."

"Oh, wow," Emma said, failing to conceal her jealousy.

There was an uncomfortable silence whilst they both thought of words to say to fill the space. There was still chemistry there, they both knew it. It was the only thing keeping them stuck to the same spot.

"So, you live close to the supermarket?" Emma asked, her own question boring her to death.

"Look, Em. I loved you. I left because we wanted different things. But I never stopped loving you. You were the love of my life."

Tears formed in Emma's eyes, her false lashes swimming, melting the glue that held them in place.

"I know. Please, don't worry. I'm so sorry I came over, I-
"

"Don't be. I wanted you to. It's good to see your face after so many years."

Emma's shoulders dropped as if a weight had been taken off her shoulders. One she'd carried around for far too long. Her entire body loosened and finally, she appeared to be comfortable.

"Thank God for that. Me to, Esther. I have really missed you. It's great to see you doing well for yourself. Who would have thought, eh? Bumping into each other here? Small world."

"Indeed. Very small."

Naturally, they both ran out of things to say, questions to ask.

"So, I'll be seeing you around, then?"

"Oh, yes, of course."

Emma turned around to leave.

"Wait, Em," Esther said.

Emma turned, trying to stop her bottom lip from trembling.

"I would love it if we could go for a coffee some time?"

"Oh, I'd love that. When are you free?"

"What about tomorrow? Afternoon?"

Emma smiled. "That sounds perfect."

They exchanged numbers. It was a date.

When Gemma arrived at the Station, she spread the images from the crime scene across her desk. She analysed for hours, the position of Emma Langley's body, each second stopping herself from associating her body with Esther. Emma's body had been screwed up and left.

It was the pink flesh, torn and suspended from the bone of her arms. The fatty tissue that burst open from her bottom lip. It bore the resemblance of burnt cream cheese. Gemma could smell it. Rotting flesh. She was taken back to the first time she'd worked on a murder case.

It was the vacant look in her eyes. That look as if life had been ripped out from her, in the same manner, her hair had been ripped from her skull, causing thin layers of flesh to peel back, matter from her brain oozing out in a gluey consistency.

TOBY'S REVENGE

Gemma knew, looking at these images that someone really hated Emma Langley. It wasn't an impulsive kill. Each puncture to the skin, each tear to her flesh was intentional and carried out with burning rage. She'd been keeping a secret and sometimes, secrets get you killed.

Mick walked into Gemma's office. His head was bowed, and his arms were tucked behind his back.

"And what do I owe this absolute pleasure?" Gemma said, appearing too occupied to acknowledge his presence.

"I'm here about the case, actually."

"Good. On the right arm of the victim, there seems to be some sort of pattern carved in. Like a weird squiggle. I can't quite make it out, so I might get Nigel to show the forensic team and see what they have to say," Gemma said whilst she rotated the image.

"Gem, what's happened?"

"Mick, I don't have the energy to get into it right now."

"Whatever it is, you know you can talk to me. It's important to talk."

Gemma let out a long sigh. She pushed the images to the side and swivelled round in her chair.

"You're right, Mick, and I will, but first, I just want to solve this case."

Mick nodded. She was right, this case had to be the primary focus.

In the pit of her stomach, Gemma knew it was the right thing to do to tell Mick about Esther's involvement with Emma Langley, but she was still her fiancé. Feelings didn't just fade away. She still felt a duty to protect Esther, from whatever trouble she could potentially face. So, she made the decision to keep this information to herself. She knew it was wrong, but what could she do? She loved her.

It was 7:45. am. Gemma was still squinting at the images of Emma Langley, with the poor assistance of her desk light. She had pondered for hours about what the mark on Emma Langley's arm could be or if it was anything at all. Maybe all the latest information about Esther had just overwhelmed her, leading her to read into everything about the case.

But as she focused more, she noticed, when titled at a 90-degree angle, the lower part of the incision made on Emma's skin. Before, she had perceived it to be some indecipherable shape, but as she took a closer look, the last part of the incision was defined, almost in the shape of the letter T. *Is that someone's initial?* Gemma thought. Maybe it was a symbol for something else, like a gang or a cult of some kind.

When Gemma next looked at the clock, it was 9: 45.pm. She had been here all day and at this rate, she was going to be here all night too. She signed off her account, gathered her things and locked the door. Tomorrow was another day and another chance to decipher some more clues.

As she made her way to the entrance, in the corner of her eye, she spotted Nigel, still researching on his computer. She hadn't noticed him at first, what with being engrossed in her own work.

"Alright, Nige," she called over to him, waving.

He waved.

"Bloody hell Gem, you scared the living shit out of me," he said, half laughing.

"Yeah, well, I think we're all a bit jumpy on this case," Gemma said.

She noticed Nigel's eagerness to close tabs on his computer.

"Eh, what are you having a gander at then?" Gemma asked, raising an eyebrow.

Nigel's face flushed a deep red.

"Gem, it's not- "

"Eh, don't play that card with me. Come on, show me, we're on the same team, aren't we?" Gemma pushed.

"It's just the phone records from Emma Langley's inbox. Text messages, so on."

Gemma frowned.

"Well, I haven't had a look yet, let's have a nose."

"Erm, Gem. Let's leave it until tomorrow, yeah?" Nigel asked, rushing to pack away his belongings.

"Nige... what's so bad about the texts?" Gemma asked. This time, her face was stone cold and serious.

"Gem come on it's late."

"No. Show me the fucking messages?" Gemma pressed.

"It's being dealt with, Gem." Nigel said, "honestly, it's nothing."

Nigel was always a terrible liar, and Gemma could always detect it.

"We had a look through her call history. We also checked her messages. We figured, with no strong leads, this would be an easier method of gathering suspects, you know? The last person she messaged might have known something."

"And? What did you find? Subscription message from Love Honey or some shite."

"Chance would be a fine thing. But no. Gem, someone was threatening Emma Langley before she died. It can't have been a one-off murder. I've got this feeling it was premeditated."

"Threatening her, how?"

"Well, we can only infer from the messages that it was over some sort of arrangement that Emma wasn't agreeing to uphold. Some sort of deal. Almost like the sender was urging her not to get in the way."

"Arrangement? I doubt a woman who got her kicks out of a finishing a Jane Austen novel for the second time was the same woman who'd be messing with the bad guys."

"Well, I guess you never really know someone," Nigel said, an expression of disappointment wiped across his face.

Esther's face came to the forefront of Gemma's mind. It loitered there like a bad smell. Those eyes she'd stared back at lovingly for seven whole years. Those eyes had become eyes she couldn't trust. She wondered if she'd ever be able to trust them again.

"Well, we've got the bloody messages. How much longer can it be until we find him?"

"Her," he blurted out.

Gemma stared at him for a couple of seconds like he was an asylum escapee.

"Her? Is that all I'm going to get?"

"It's a *her*, Gem. We believe the killer is a woman or at least a woman who assisted the killer. There were... pictures, of a woman. Suggestive ones. We think maybe Emma could have been cheating on her husband with another woman."

For the briefest of moments, Gemma didn't quite process what Nigel had just said.

"Oh yeah, well. I always did have my suspicions about Mrs Brown, the cheeky old bat. Wouldn't put it past her after that incident at the Post Office. Using Dementia as an excuse for stealing, stealthy even for an OAP, eh?"

The smirk that usually smeared its way across Nigel's face whenever Gemma cracked a joke failed to appear. Gemma waited patiently for it to save her from the moment, but the moment went on for too long. It began to feel like a huge stone had sunk, sunk and landed at the pit of Gemma's stomach.

"Nige? You're not joking... are you?"

Nigel threw Gemma a glance and, in that moment, she knew that eyes revealed more truth than words ever could.

Light spilled in through the open blinds. Gemma's sleep was interrupted by the clinking together of mugs. Then it hit her. She was still engaged to a liar. She'd hoped so much that this was all a nightmare.

She could sense from the fumbling around that Esther had realised just how wrong she had been. Guilt would often cause her to be a little clumsier than usual.

"Morning, babe. How are you feeling?" Esther asked, putting on her customer service voice.

The tension was palpable. Gemma turned onto her back and stared at the ceiling.

"Look Gem, I'm not trying to say that I'm right about any of this, far from it, but what I want you to know is that I love you. I want to marry you."

"Marriage has vows involved, Esther. Vows of trust. The trust you've succeeded in breaking."

"Gem, please. You can't punish me forever."

"Watch me."

"Well, I think I should be given a second chance. After all, my intention was to protect you."

"What if some people are only supposed to be given one chance in life and if they mess that one up, there's no turning back? tell me something, my darling fiancé," Gemma spat, flipping her body around and sitting upright, "When were you actually last in contact with Mrs Langley?"

At that moment, Esther would have done anything for the world to swallow her up.

"God, Gem I don't know... ages ago in passing."

Gemma chucked her head back. She laughed so hard it could have been mistaken for some sort of seizure.

"You really expect me to believe that? After what I've discovered? What's to say you're not hiding more?"

Quicker than it takes to boil a kettle, Esther's mug smashed against the wall. The Duvet was ripped from Gemma's body like a band-aid from her skin. Esther was closer to Gemma than the last breath she exhaled.

"Esther," Gemma whispered.

Esther gave no response. Two black voids for eyes gazed into Gemma's, swallowing her oxygen. Gemma wondered why the hell life had turned out this way for her. She was desperate to know what she had ever done in her past life to deserve this.

"What the fuck, Esther!" Gemma shouted, pushing Esther back.

Esther blinked. Short and sharp, like she'd been in a trance. She did it for a few seconds. Then, she took a deep breath through her nose and exhaled out of her mouth. She collapsed on the floor and stared up at Gemma.

A moment of silence filled the space between them.

"What the fuck just happened?"

Esther was despondent. Her arms were loosely folded, and her head remained bowed in despair.

"You know, I can't believe this shit. What the fuck is happening? What do you know that you're not telling me?"

"I don't know what you're talking about."

"You know something, Esther. I will find out what it is you're hiding."

"Oh yeah? Well, it took you a while to figure this one out, so I doubt it."

"What is that supposed to mean?"

Esther sighed. She seemed angry with herself. It was almost like she'd given away too much.

"You know something, don't you?"

"Of course not, Gem. I'm just grieving."

"You and me both," Gemma said, looking Esther up and down like she was a stranger in her home.

BEFORE THE MURDER

ESTHER

When she got back home, Esther laid the shopping out on the counter and opened the cupboards with the intention of putting it all away. But she was far too occupied with thoughts of Emma.

She couldn't get her head around the fact that Emma had been in Oakley Green, in the same supermarket as her. She looked exactly the same, but better. She'd aged well. Esther reminisced on the feeling of running her fingers through that long silky hair of hers when they made love. She remembered the way Em kissed her, so tender, so pure. They had something special. Something rarer than anyone else had.

She sat at the kitchen table, scrolled through the contacts on her phone and hovered over **Emma**. She had to change the name, in case Gemma saw it. But, what would she change it to so that she would remember as well?

E. Would be too risky, far too obvious, and how would she explain that?

She spent the afternoon trying to think of names she could use instead of **Emma**. She could possibly pretend that this was a work colleague? Someone who had just started? But then, why would she be texting her so much.

Oh, God. She had to do it. It would be so weird, but it was the only way it would look normal.

She saved **Emma** as **Mum X** instead. That way Gemma wouldn't become too suspicious.

With butterflies in her stomach, she prepared the first text, her heartbeat correlating with the flickering of the cursor on the screen.

`Hi, Em. It's Esther. I just wanted to say that it was great seeing you earlier. I` really am happy for you. Still on for that coffee tomorrow? X

Sent.

Esther sat there, giddy and excited like a child over their crush. Could this be a sign that their relationship wasn't over? She knew that she and Gemma were due to be married in a year's time, but part of her still loved Emma. It always would. Emma coming back into Esther's life really shook everything up.

BEFORE THE MURDER

EMMA

When Emma packed her shopping away and got back into the car, she felt a wave of relief. She took a deep breath, taking it all in. God, she was still like Emma remembered her. She was still naturally gorgeous. Her voice was warm and calming. Esther was a piece of familiarity that she'd been missing from the puzzle that was her life.

I wonder if just a text wouldn't hurt? Emma thought. In the back of her mind, she felt guilty because of Dave. But he didn't pay her any attention, taking calls every five minutes, barely trying it on with her. Today was the first time she'd felt that excitement she'd longed for.

Two minutes later, she received a text. It was from Esther.

Hi, Em. It's Esther. I just wanted to say that it was great seeing you earlier. I really am happy for you. Still on for that coffee tomorrow? X

Oh, *God*. She messaged first. That was a relief. Emma hated texting first. She'd always felt like she was aggravating the other person, or that she was desperate for wanting to start the conversation. She was glad. She was glad that Esther reciprocated the feelings she had.

After a minute spent on what to reply back, Emma wrote:

Hey, Esther. It was great seeing you too, you seem really happy. I would love to go for coffee. Looking forward to it. Is 1: 00.pm okay? Xx

Sent.

TOBY'S REVENGE

Oh, shit. Two kisses! She hadn't meant to do that. Bloody autocorrect.

BEFORE THE MURDER

ESTHER

It was a pleasant morning. The sun was beaming over Oakley Green, Gemma was downstairs making them both coffees and the bath was running. Later Esther would be meeting Emma for a coffee. She thought of this whilst sipping on the one Gemma had just brought up to her.

"You don't mind if I work late tonight, do you, babe?" Gemma called from the bathroom.

Esther took another sip of her coffee, grinning, "No babe, of course not. Go and catch the baddies."

Gemma came back through to the bedroom, drenched in Invictus, kissing Esther on the lips and making her way out the door.

"You're the best babe. Love you, see you later!"

"Bye, babe, love you," Esther called back, waiting for the slamming of the front door.

The house fell silent. Esther liked it that way. She could hear her thoughts properly without interruption or distraction.

What would she wear today? She wanted to look nice for Emma. She wanted her to think about what she'd missed out on all these years ago.

After trying on a million different outfits, she finally decided on one. A tight black bodycon number. It hugged her in all the right places, accentuating her curves and framing her breasts. She topped off the look with a large pearl necklace and a beige camel coat. Classy was the look she was aiming for. Emma loved classy. She'd always looked expensive in everything she wore.

Now for the makeup. She didn't want to overdo it. She didn't want Emma thinking that Esther had made all this effort just to impress her. She wanted to appear as though she'd already been out, running errands, a chic windswept kind of appearance.

On her skin, she used BB cream in the shade Light Beige, nothing too overpowering. It was natural. Next, a thin layer of black eyeliner to bring out the green in her eyes, two strokes of Rimmel XXL Lashes Mascara and for the lips, a subtle but classic nude shade Lipstick from MAC.

BEFORE THE MURDER

EMMA

Fuck, fuck, fuck. Emma was experiencing the worst of bad hair days. It was typical. When she wanted to look her most glamorous, for events, or dinner, the process never seemed to run smoothly, but when she was sitting on the sofa with Dave doing absolutely nothing, she looked fabulous, beautiful. She wanted to look beautiful today.

Coffee with Esther. Coffee with Esther. Coffee with Esther. She repeated it in her head all the way home. She'd found it quite thrilling that she was keeping a secret from Dave, who was none the wiser.

She'd spent all of last night laying out the perfect outfit. She chose a classic black suit and low-cut white blouse to put underneath. She wanted a bit of cleavage to be on show. After all, she hadn't had the opportunity to flaunt it in a while, being cooped up in the house, and at the school, she had to dress appropriately because of the children. She couldn't risk giving off the wrong impression. It was high neck jumpers and tailored trousers every day of the week.

They'd agreed to meet at a small independent coffee shop just around the corner from the school. Hopefully, none of her students would spot her. There was something so strange about speaking to her students outside of school hours. It was like she felt awkward about telling them off that day because they weren't in her classroom.

For an hour, she'd practiced how she was going to greet Esther and what she would say, how she would open the conversation. Would she begin talking about her job as a teacher, or would that be too boring?

She wasn't sure, but what she did know was that she was incredibly nervous.

Esther was the first to arrive at the coffee shop. She'd ordered a medium latte, no sugar. She still got the same order, nothing had changed.

"I took the liberty of ordering you an iced coffee, it's still your favourite, I hope?" She asked, wincing.

Emma smiled, took her coat off and sat down beside her.

"Oh yes, it still is, thanks."

Emma couldn't help but stare at Esther in awe. She was truly beautiful, and naturally so. Dave crossed her mind for a brief second, but he soon faded away once Esther opened her mouth the speak.

"You look lovely. Still so glowing, I always wondered how you managed it."

Butterflies were circling in Emma's stomach. Esther thought *she* was lovely? She hadn't received a compliment in a long time. It felt nice.

"Aw, thank-you, ditto. I love your lipstick, is it MAC? Amazing coverage."

"Yes, it is actually. Only the best. You never know when you'll need to pucker up."

Emma's cheeks reddened at the thought of kissing Esther's lips.

"So," Emma started, changing the conversation, what is it that you do for work now? I never asked you."

"Oh, nothing too amazing, I'm doing admin for Oakley Green College a few miles away. Just an assistant."

Emma slurped her coffee, trying her hardest to look impressed.

"What do you do? I bet you're a makeup artist or a model or something."

Emma giggled.

"No! I actually got a job teaching English at the school down the road, Le Petit Oak?"

"No way! *You're* a teacher? We used to take the piss out of teachers together."

Emma laughed, putting her head in her hands.

"I know, I know! It just happened."

"Wow, Em. That's amazing. Do you actually enjoy it?"

"I mean, it's rewarding for sure, but some of the students get right on my nerves. Especially one of the boys I teach, Toby. He's a bloody nightmare and apparently, from what I hear, his father was the same."

"Oh, really? See, I couldn't deal with that. All those snotty children in one classroom misbehaving. I'd pull my hair out; I don't know how you do it Em."

"Well, you know. It's a job, I suppose they're all stressful in their own way."

"So, this boy, how bad is he?"

Emma rolled her eyes, taking a gulp of her iced coffee.

"I mean, I shouldn't really say, but he's awful, Esther. He just doesn't listen to me, he tells me to fuck off, he's a troubled kid. He doesn't like me, that's for sure. I have a feeling it's because I'm one of the new kids on the block."

"Oh, well, fuck him, the little bastard."

Emma gasped, laughing hard. It was funnier because it was so forbidden.

"So, what are you doing after this?" Esther asked, tipping her coffee cup up so that all was visible were her eyes.

Her mysterious, beautiful eyes that glistened in the natural light like rare gems.

"Oh, well you know, I've got some work to mark. Teacher life," she lied.

"I hope you don't think I'm being too forward. I know we haven't seen each other in years, but it feels like yesterday that we were hanging out together."

Emma's desire to lean over and kiss Esther was burning. She knew it was wrong, but she couldn't help herself.

"I just wondered if maybe you wanted to come to mine for a quick glass of wine? For old time's sake? I mean we have just been drinking coffee, but it's wine o'clock somewhere, right?"

"Oh, well you know I shouldn't really, I've got an absolute mountain of papers to mark and they won't mark themselves," Emma declined, thinking to herself about how boring she must have sounded, how boring she must have become over the years.

"Oh, no it's fine, just an idea," Esther said, pretending she wasn't bothered.

"Well, I suppose one glass wouldn't hurt, would it?" Emma asked, desperately seeking reassurance that intending to cheat on her husband was completely fine.

"Oh, no, one glass is perfectly acceptable. I promise," Esther said, grinning. It felt like they had reconnected again.

BEFORE THE MURDER

EMMA

Fuck, what am I doing? I'd be furious if this were Dave, Emma said to herself as she waited for Esther to go and get some wine out from the garage. She did feel guilty, she really did, but spending time with Esther made her feel alive. She felt fun.

Esther made her way back in, locking the door behind her.

"Where's your fiancé? I'd love to meet her one time?" Emma lied.

"Oh, she's at work. She's a Detective, so sometimes she works until quite late," Esther said, popping the cork of the wine bottle. Something about being here with Esther alone made Emma feel so devious. It was like they were committing some sort of crime.

Esther grabbed two pristine wine glasses, placed them on coasters and began pouring the wine.

"Do you mind if I go and get changed into something more comfortable? Sorry, I'm just feeling quite uncomfortable in this dress."

"Oh, of course, that's fine. I'll just be drinking this," Emma smiled.

When Esther made her way upstairs, Emma took it as an opportunity to snoop. She wanted to know what Esther's fiancé looked like. She wandered over to the hallway to see if there were any pictures. There weren't.

The decoration of the house was all in all, quite dull, grey walls, silver and grey ornaments, grey and white kitchen counters and cupboards. It could have passed for a show home. Not like hers, Dave's underwear thrown on the sofa, soaking wet towels left, sprawled across the soggy bathmat. Food and plates left out in the kitchen piled higher than their martial issues.

Emma was startled by Esther coming down the stairs. She quickly made her way back into the kitchen, sitting back where she had been, pretending she hadn't been snooping.

When Esther strutted into the kitchen, Emma's heart skipped a beat. She came down wearing the most beautifully embroidered lingerie, a silk robe tied around the middle of her waist, though not tight enough to stop rest of her body from spilling out.

"You like it?" Esther asked, staring straight into Emma's eyes.

Emma's knees went weak.

"You're beautiful," She said, pushing her wine to one side.

"Would you mind helping me take it off?" Esther asked, her eyes darting towards the stairs.

Enough was enough. It was time to stop playing games. They wanted each other and they always had. Emma tried to keep up pretences, but she couldn't stand it anymore. She wasn't happy with Dave. With Esther, she felt happy. It was like they'd never been apart.

Emma walked over to Esther, stared at her for a few seconds whilst stroking her hair. She looked into those eyes of hers and melted.

"Let's finish what we started," Emma whispered. She threw Esther against the wall, caressing her body, kissing her violently.

They made their way upstairs, got into bed and made love for hours.

"Wow, I guess you did miss me," Esther said, laughing.

"So much," Emma said, looking back at her with pure happiness.

BEFORE THE MURDER

TOBY

Toby hated Mrs Langley. She was such a boring bitch, and a slag too. Always wearing clothes too tight for her. Did she not realise that it came across as extremely desperate? She knew what she was doing.

Last week she gave him a detention for asking if she was married. It was a simple question, but of course, she's so self-centred that she interpreted it the wrong way. I wonder often how she got into teaching, whether she took the academic route, or fucked her way to the top.

She's always singled me out, tried to make a fool out of me, but she doesn't know my history. She doesn't know where I come from. She's just moved here, so of course, she needs educating on the history of Oakley Green. She never knew my father and if she did, she wouldn't be treating me this way. He'd have told her where to go, her and her Botox-filled face.

She better not cross me again, and if she does, they'll be consequences.

BEFORE THE MURDER

GEMMA

This past couple of weeks, Esther had been distant around her. She couldn't understand what she'd done wrong if anything at all. She couldn't exactly use the excuse that it was just a woman thing. She'd make them dinner tonight; finish work early and get to the bottom of why she was acting so peculiarly.

Was she working too much? Did Esther feel like she wasn't giving her enough attention?

It was driving her insane, all these assumptions, no facts.

But that's what she did best. Find the facts, and tonight, she would.

BEFORE THE MURDER

ESTHER

They were meeting up again tonight after Emma had finished work. Esther was going to meet her in the car park at the School. They'd been seeing each other for a couple of months now and each time, the passion grew.

They were going to drive away somewhere for a few hours later and have some time to themselves. It was so wrong, but it felt so exhilarating. It felt enjoyable to share a secret, to be sharing a sin. If you got into trouble, if anyone found out, you knew that the other person was in exactly the same position as you were. You had each other, though, it wouldn't be as exciting.

Esther was getting ready in the bathroom. Gemma said she'd be working until after midnight, so they had hours.

As she was getting out of the shower, her phone vibrated violently on her dresser. It was a text from Emma.

Last night was AMAZING. Can't wait to see you later. X

She swelled with excitement, unable to resist grinning stupidly at her phone. She typed a message and sent it. This time, she sent a picture of her breasts.

Can't wait to see you later. Will be so much fun. X

Sent.

Almost immediately, Emma replied with a love-struck face emoji.

Lol, I'm working! Looking hot though. X

It was so much fun, seeing Emma. Esther adored her and always had, though, recently, she had felt that maybe she

TOBY'S REVENGE

was trying too hard to get back what they had years before.

Could they turn back time?

BEFORE THE MURDER

EMMA

Emma could hardly contain her excitement at the image Esther had sent her. It all felt so forbidden, especially whilst she was sitting there, marking papers with her students in front of her.

She was having the time of her life with Esther. Who would have thought they'd ever see each other again, after years of being apart and knowing nothing about each other? It had to be fate, them meeting again like this. Emma knew it was. She could feel it. What were the odds that Esther would have been at the supermarket that day? And how had they not bumped into each other sooner? It was impossible.

Even so, she was glad they did. It was the best thing that had happened to her in a long time. She was happier and that was all that mattered, even if she would be hurting David in the long run.

She wished she didn't have to sit here marking papers for another two hours. She'd rather be out with Esther, laughing and joking, holding her in her arms, reminiscing on the old days.

That little shit Toby kept staring at her. He sat in the front row, arms folded, the look of anger on his that made him appear older than he was.

"Toby, if you've finished your assignment, you should go back through your answers and double check them with the remaining time you have left."

He didn't answer. Instead, he picked his nose and wiped it across the paper he'd written his answers on.

"Toby, that's disgusting. Go and wash your hands, please."

"How about this, Mrs Langley? How about, you stop being a bitch, and I'll go and wash my hands."

There was a gasp from the students.

"Toby, go to Miss Skitter's office. Perhaps you'd feel more comfortable talking to her about why your behaviour had become so poor."

"Perhaps I wouldn't. Bitch."

Emma slammed her pen down, pushed her chair out and stormed over to Toby's desk. She snatched his paper and held it up to show the class what he had done.

"If anyone else would like to spend the rest of their lunchtimes this week in detention, I suggest you follow in Mr. Devourt's footsteps."

There was silence in the classroom.

Emma leaned down so that she was at Toby's level.

TOBY'S REVENGE

"Unfortunately, Toby, we are unable to accept rubbish, what a shame. Your mother and father will be so very disappointed," She said, getting up and tossing Toby's assignment carelessly into the bin.

"Apologies everyone, please carry on with your assignments," she said, darting a look of disgust Toby's way.

BEFORE THE MURDER

TOBY

Toby's rage was bubbling up. Heat rose within him. *How dare she*. She wasn't allowed to behave that way. He'd show her.

He'd report her immediately. It was *his* piece of work and he was allowed to do what he wanted with it. If he wanted to take a shit on it, he would have.

She was treading on thin ice. Anymore cracks, and she would sink.

BEFORE THE MURDER

ESTHER

Why was Gemma ringing her again? Wasn't she supposed to be working? Esther kept ignoring her calls, hoping she'd give up. She did, eventually and left a voicemail.

"Hey, babe, it's me. Look, I know I've been really tied up with work these past few weeks, but I really want to make it up to you. How about dinner tonight? A couple of bottles of wine? Just me and you? I've got to get back to work, but I love you. Bye."

It wasn't that Esther didn't appreciate the fact that Gemma had recognised her downfall, it was just that she didn't really feel anything for her anymore. It sounded awful and evil, but it was true. She just felt, sort of detached from her. Like all the food times they had together were in the past and there to stay. She had no intention of responding to the voicemail. The only intention she had was to meet with Emma and have an amazing night.

Anyway, she was nearly on her way to the School and she could see Emma's metallic blue Peugeot parked at the front. Thirty minutes and she'd be finished. Esther didn't mind waiting.

She thought maybe she ought to leave Gemma a message back, out of respect. She'd tell her she was sorry and that she couldn't make it because she was helping with some extra projects at work. That seemed plausible.

Thirty minutes had passed. Esther was waiting in the same position by one of the trees at the School gate. She watched as swarms of teenagers piled out of the double doors, getting their phones out immediately after not being allowed to use them for a whole day.

She walked forward, blending in with the crowd of parents waiting at the gate to pick their kids up.

Straight ahead, she saw Emma in her classroom, packing things away. She ran over, tapped on the window and pulled a silly face. Emma looked up, startled and then, realising it was Esther, laughed hysterically.

There was a young boy in her classroom sitting at the back. Miserable little thing. Had a face like a slapped arse.

Who's that? Esther mouthed to Emma.

Emma rolled her eyes, grinned and held her index finger up.

Esther waited near Emma's car, cautiously keeping the lookout for nosy parents.

BEFORE THE MURDER

EMMA

"Toby, I'm just going to pack some things away and then I'll leave you in peace, okay?" Emma said, rushing around so that she could get out of this hell hole and meet Esther.

"You don't finish for another ten minutes," Toby said, pointing at the clock.

Emma sighed.

"What is it with you, Toby? Why can't you just be polite? None of the other kids act up the way you do? Is it something I've done?"

Toby didn't say a word. He just shot Emma a look of hatred that penetrated through her, sending a shiver down her spine and up her neck.

She couldn't lie. She was scared of him. It was something about him, the atmosphere he created whenever he was present. She wondered, could it truly be possible for someone to be evil? Was it really nurture over nature?

Toby Devourt was prompting her to challenge this.

BEFORE THE MURDER

TOBY

As Emma left, Toby watched her until she got to her car which he could see clearly from the classroom window. He watched her as she piled books into the back of her boot, shut it and made her way around. Then, out of the blue, a woman with long brown hair came jumping out of the bush next to the car, scaring Emma.

Toby observed Emma's face. The fear in it. It pleased him, to see her so frightened, in a state of vulnerability.

He watched on as this woman came up behind Emma, kissed her on the neck, played with her hair and made her way into the car. They drove off, appearing to be more than friends.

TOBY'S REVENGE

But, wasn't Mrs Langley married? Toby thought, *to a* man?

BEFORE THE MURDER

GEMMA

She's staying late at work? But, why? She never really did that. Perhaps it was just a one-off. *What if she is seeing someone else?* Gemma questioned. Then, feeling guilty for even suggesting it, she shrugged it off and went into the kitchen to make a drink.

"Pasta for one then," she said, disappointed.

She made her way into the living room. There was no point sitting at the table if it was only going to be her. She'd be a slob tonight. Sprawl out on the couch, stick a good film on and stuff her face with carbs. That's how you do it. That's how you *really* make yourself feel better.

Esther would be back soon enough and she'd have nothing to be worried about. She trusted her fiancé, and she should have all along. Esther had never given her any reason to doubt her before. It was just good old-fashioned paranoia, creeping in at the first sign of trouble. It had to be. Esther would never betray her like that, would she?

BEFORE THE MURDER

ESTHER

They drove to a random field just outside of town and made love all night, blasting out old songs on Emma's shitty car stereo.

"Do you really have to go back home to your fiancé?" Emma said, frowning.

"Do you *really* have to go back home to your *husband*?" Emma replied.

They both sat there in fits of laughter, relishing their little secret.

"No, but seriously," Emma said, "do you think we will ever be together one day? Like we were?"

Esther began to feel the fun slip away. It was all this talk about reality and seriousness. It was dampened her mood.

"Oh, I don't know, Em. I mean, we've had a good run, haven't we? We've had fun?"

Emma's face screwed up. She moved away from Esther abruptly.

"What's that supposed to mean?"

Esther sighed.

"I didn't mean anything by it. I just mean that- "

"You just mean that I was a little project for you. Something to do on the side of your actual life?" Emma interrupted, tears forming in her eyes.

"Oh Em, please don't make this bigger than it is."

"I really don't mean anything to you, do I? You never really gave a shit about me in the first place, did you? I was just something to pass the time."

"Oh, come on. You're being ridiculous. Of course, I care about you. I'm with you now, aren't I?"

"Yes, and then you'll go back to your fiancé who bores the life out of you and pretend to be in love," Emma spat.

Esther put her arm on Emma's shoulder. She shook it off.

"Look, Em, all I'm trying to say is, can't we just keep having fun? Can't we just continue doing what we're doing?"

"So, you want me to pretend I don't love you. You want me to pretend that I'm happy for you when I see you and your fiancé out together?"

"*Love*? What about your husband?"

"What about your fiancé!? You're just as bad as I am."

This was a complete mess and Esther knew it. Things had gone too far. She knew it the first moment she saw Emma in the supermarket. Her coming back into her life was bad news.

"So, what do you think should happen? Should I break up with Gemma and you break up with Dave and then we get together and live happily ever after?"

Emma sobbed against the steering wheel dramatically, as she always did when they argued.

"Emma, please don't cry."

"Fuck you."

"Hey, don't take this out on me, it takes two to tango."

"Let's tell your fiancé. Let's tell her tonight."

Esther froze, dread coursing through her body.

"Are you insane, Em? No."

"If you were serious about me, you'd tell her. She deserves to know."

Esther grabbed Emma by the shoulders, shaking her.

"I said no, Emma. Gemma is not allowed to know what has gone on between us, okay?"

"Why not? Why are you so afraid of her knowing?"

"Because she's my fucking fiancé. We share a house together, we have commitments. I'm not about to throw that all away for- "

Tears fell down Emma's cheeks.

"I understand."

"Emma, I'm sorry. I didn't mean to say that."

"Oh, I think you did."

They drove back home in complete silence. All that was audible was Emma's sobbing.

BEFORE THE MURDER

GEMMA

"What time did you get in last night?" Gemma asked, rolling over to face Esther who was flicking through her phone.

"About quarter to eleven. Sorry if I woke you, babe. The college wanted me to help with this huge project. At least it's more money."

"Oh, no worries babe. Just got worried that's all. What was it? The project?" Gemma asked, treading carefully so she didn't sound too suspicious.

"Oh, nothing. Just some sculpture thing that one of the Art students is working on. Needed extra materials, that sort of thing," Emma said, wincing at how weak the lie was.

"Oh, sounds interesting. I missed you last night. I was looking forward to spending some time with you. I know I've been busy lately but, I still care about. I love you, Esther Quinn."

Esther smiled back, rubbing Gemma's face. But she couldn't help it. Every time she looked at Gemma, she saw Emma.

"We can do it another night? Dinner?"

"What about tonight?" Gemma asked.

"Erm, yeah that should be fine," Esther said, kissing Gemma on the forehead, feeling Emma's smooth skin on her lips, the sweet scent of her hair.

"Good. Can't wait," Gemma said, jumping out of bed enthusiastically, "Do you want a coffee babe?" She called.

TOBY'S REVENGE

She needed more than a bloody coffee. She needed about ten litres of vodka to forget about this slip-up.

"Yes, please. Coffee would be perfect."

BEFORE THE MURDER

TOBY

Toby watched as Mrs Langley made her way into class the next day. The classroom was empty and the English lesson wasn't due to begin for another thirty minutes.

Her eyes were puffy like she'd been crying. *Probably had something to do with her girlfriend,* he supposed. He was right about her. She was a slag. Cheating on her husband with that woman. She should be ashamed of herself. Usually, it was the other way around and people would blame the man for running off with someone else. But this just proved that women are as bad if not worse.

"Mrs Langley, you look awfully distraught. Whatever could be the matter on such a lovely day?" Toby asked, smirking.

"Not today, Toby. Anyway, your lesson doesn't start for another half an hour," Emma snapped, brushing through sheets of paper on her desk.

"Nothing to do with your girlfriend, is it?"

Emma froze.

"What did you just say?"

"Well, I wasn't going to mention it, but it's just that, I was curious because yesterday evening when you put me in detention for absolutely nothing, I saw you outside by your car, canoodling with a woman. Only, I thought you were married, Mrs Langley, to a man?" Toby asked, a smug grin spread from ear to ear.

Emma began playing nervously with her hair, winding it tight around her finger until it turned purple.

"Oh, her. No, Toby, you seem to be mistaken. Esther's an old friend of mine. We met in Paris when we were teenagers. She dropped by to say hello."

"Oh, my apologies, Mrs Langley, it's just that I distinctly remember seeing her kiss you on the neck. Perhaps I need my eyes tested."

Emma began to tear up.

"Oh, don't cry, Mrs Langley. There are plenty more lesbians in the sea."

"Get out!" She screamed, tears falling from her eyes, hitting the floor.

BEFORE THE MURDER

EMMA

That little shit. She knew she shouldn't let him get to her, but today, she couldn't tolerate his manipulative ways. She was hurting. Now that she and Esther were essentially over.

She needed to speak to her. Esther needed to see how in love they were. She wasn't thinking rationally. There was no way Emma was prepared to let what they had go, for the sake of a house, or a car, or money. She loved Esther with her whole heart. She couldn't live with knowing that she did nothing to fight for their relationship.

If Esther was going to refuse to talk to her, she'd have to tell Gemma. It was the only way they could be together. Once

Gemma knew, she'd kick Esther out. Esther would have no choice but to be with her.

They could go far away from Oakley Green, off into the sunset and have their happy ever after like they should have had all along.

Gemma was the only thing getting in the way. Emma needed to get her out of the picture and fast.

AFTER THE MURDER: THE INVESTIGATION

GEMMA

Mick was standing there like a bulldog, guarding its territory when Gemma arrived at work.

"I think it's best if you step into the office, Gem."

"Oh Mick, really? I mean I know I've been a mardy cow recently, but does it really call for the treatment?"

Mick remained silent.

In the corner of her eye, Gemma could see Nigel peeping through the blinds in the office window. Other colleagues congregated to get their fill of the latest piece of drama. There was a look of regret and disappointment on Nigel's face.

Gemma proceeded to make her way into Mick's office.

"What's going on? Why is everyone staring?"

"Gem, how are you feeling?"

"Oh yeah, great."

Mick ignored Gemma and turned his attention to the old image of Oakley Green. His face dropped.

"You know, from a young age I knew I wanted to be on the force."

"If you've got a point to make Mick, I suggest you make it sharpish," Gemma snapped.

There was a faint knock at the door. As the doorknob turned, Gemma could sense from the awkward rattling, combined with the repetition of weakly executed coughs, it was Nigel.

"Ah, Nigel. Take a seat," Mick said, gesturing to the seat beside Gemma.

Nigel nodded and sat like an obedient puppy, "alright Gem?"

Gemma stared at him. She did so for a few seconds too long to make him feel uncomfortable.

"Right," Gemma said, turning to Mick and then back to Nigel, "Does someone want to tell me what's going on? Or do I dare do what I'm paid to do and investigate?"

"Stop, Gem," Mick barked.

Gemma jumped up in her seat.

"Excuse me?"

Nigel and Mick exchanged looks.

"Gemma, with regret, I must ask you whether you know the identity of the person who killed Emma Langley, or if you were involved in any way?"

It was clear now that to suggest this was a prank was not just a stab, but a massacre in the dark. The gravity of Mick's question was undeniable.

Gemma attempted to mouth the words she wanted to say, but no sound came out.

"I'm sorry, Gem, but if you know anything..."

"How dare you," Gemma seethed, "what is going on here?"

Whilst Mick fumbled around, Gemma turned to Nigel, shaking her head in disbelief.

"And you. I thought we were friends. You think I can chop people up, do you? I can barely chop up a bloody turkey for Christmas dinner."

"Gem, please. It's just... the evidence we've obtained from Emma Langley's phone records, suggests that you might have known or assisted the killer. You're mentioned, you see, in the messages."

TOBY'S REVENGE

Gemma's pulse was thumping in her ears. The muscles in her jaws jumped through her skin. How dare they question her integrity. How dare they even entertain the idea of her being involved in a brutal crime such as this.

Once Mick handed the evidence to Gemma, which she snatched off him, there were a series of text messages between two parties. However, both had remained anonymous. The texts read:

07536789032: YOU'RE WRONG. GEMMA WILL ALWAYS DEFEND ME. SHE'S BEEN ON MY SIDE FROM THE BEGINNING. WHEN YOU'RE DEALT WITH, SHE'LL REJOICE WITH ME.

07586993495: You can't do this Est. If you don't tell her the truth, I will. She's a Detective for goodness sake! She'll find out the truth. She must have suspected?

07536789032: EXACTLY. BUT SHE'LL FORGIVE ME. YOU'LL BE GONE AND FORGOTTEN.

Gemma read with horror. Goosebumps formed up her arms. Who would have done this to her? Set her up like this?

"Gem. I know this is hard."

"It's not what you think," Gemma gushed, tears in her eyes, "I swear, I don't know anything about this, Mick."

"Gem, do you have any idea why someone would mention you in these texts? Any information you've been concealing?"

Gemma dropped her head and let out a sigh.

"What is it?" Nigel asked.

"I was going to tell you, Mick, I was."

"Tell me what?" Mick stared, his eyebrows looming over like two fat furry caterpillars.

"Esther. It's Esther, she told me that she knew Emma from years ago. She said she'd seen her in the supermarket and Emma had told her she moved here with her husband for work. I think they dated for a while."

Mick shook his head, throwing it into both hands.

"Mick, I'm sorry. I was going to say something I swear. I've just been busy with all the other details of the case. I wanted to forget about it and do my job."

"Forget about it?! Gem, this information could have helped us."

"I know, I'm sorry, but if I thought for a second that Esther was involved in the case, I would have taken her in myself. She was distraught, Mick. She promised she'd only seen her in passing."

Taking a look at the messages again, Gemma's face changed, angry this time, mixed with shock.

"What is it?"

Gemma's mouth went dry. Her limbs felt weak.

"It's... it's the first phone number. I-I didn't see it a minute ago, but, but I know it," Gemma was shaking, head to toe.

Mick's face was the off-white colour of old kitchen appliances.

Nigel's eyes bulged.

"The, the first number. It's Esther. It's Esther's mobile number," Gemma blurted out, gripping the piece of paper.

"You're sure?" Mick asked.

Gemma froze. She couldn't bring herself to say a word. This just couldn't be happening. First, Esther lied to her about knowing Emma, and then this? She *had* been in contact with Emma. She lied. Gemma should have known. All those late-night texts, all the times Esther said it was her Mum checking in on her. It was Emma. They were having an affair right under her nose.

"Oh God, Gem, you should have informed me of this," Mick said, "you know what we have to do."

"I'm so sorry," Gemma managed, before breaking down into Nigel's arms.

For what felt like hours, Gemma watched in awe like the rest of the passers-by. That way, she was able to pretend this wasn't her life. She watched as her colleagues turned up at her and Esther's home, broke down the door that Esther had picked out when they were house hunting together.

She observed Esther's face. That unique expression of pure fear and yet slight relief on a person's face when they realise, they've been caught, the truth exposed.

The world she and Esther had built, the one she considered to be solid and concrete, was now being demolished before her eyes. She watched on, every scene, pressing against her like an unforgiving, relentless tide.

"Gem?! Gemma please," Esther shouted, pushing back against one of the officers.

She cried through the drama, although, her efforts were futile. Her voice was a blur to Gemma. It was merely a grain in the gargantuan barrel of despair she found herself in.

Once Esther had been escorted dramatically away to the Station for questioning, Gemma had nothing else to do but think. Think about what to do next, think about how to carry on, think about why the fuck she let Esther pick those curtains in that shade in the lounge. She'd be better off keeping busy, she knew that, but she couldn't face going back to work yet. She couldn't stand the thought of everyone believing she was in on it, like it was her dirty little secret she had been keeping for Esther.

***

It had been two days since Esther's arrest. Two days of Gemma battling the urge to down a bottle of wine, or three.

She could taste that burnt oak at the back of her throat. That sharp scent of Merlot clinging to the insides of her nostrils. A drink that, once upon a time, she and Esther drank together.

The feeling that Gemma felt when she drank was one, she couldn't explain. She'd had no worry in the world. She felt no pain. That feeling was difficult to forget, difficult to give up. And that's where she supposed, her addiction began.

Taking it back to a day in the life of a young Gemma McCarthy: a bombardment of montages consisting of her mother's eye sockets, never changing from the colour combination of deep purple and charcoal black. Doors slamming. Expletives tossed around like frisbees.

Her father was a piece of shit. She knew it. Everyone knew it. Thing is, no one did anything about it. And why the fuck would they? It wasn't their problem. So, Gemma supposed at nine years old, it was her problem. If no one was going to be bothered to protect her mother, she would.

TOBY'S REVENGE

Despite her efforts, despite taking on this new indestructible, heroine role, the beatings grew increasingly worse. Gemma was only so strong and could only hold her father back so much, and even then, she'd always get caught in the crossfire. Unexplained bruises, cuts. Teachers were increasingly suspicious by the day. But they didn't know the battle she was facing, day in, day out. They could judge her all the liked. She knew she was the stronger one and would be in the end.

When secondary school came around, Gemma started going to the gym. She became physically stronger, stronger even than most of the guys in her year. But, inevitably, the beatings got worse. Gemma realised that she simply couldn't afford to invest time in her studies. She had bigger problems to solve, scarier monsters than the ones mentioned in the books she had to read for English class. So, she stayed home. She kept her father away, if only for short while.

The toll it took on her was enormous. As time passed by, Gemma came to the realisation that no matter how long she tried to keep her mother safe, her father would always make his way back, and the tragedy was, her mother would always let him back in. Gemma couldn't take it. She turned to alcohol and never turned back. It was the beginning of a dangerous love affair.

But just as she was drowning and choking on life like an oppressive tide covering the shore, that's when she met Esther. Esther was the antidote. She was the erasure of the cruelty that addiction inevitably dragged with it.

It had always been Gemma's intention to join the police. Once upon a time, she'd wanted to be a Detective. But, as usual, life proceeded to act as the splinter in flesh, her pain stopping her from chasing her dreams.

It was only two months later that Gemma met Mick. She didn't believe in fate. Who could blame her? Fate just didn't happen to someone like her. Everything that had happened to her was thrown, with an intentional permanence she couldn't shake off.

On that night before meeting Mick, Gemma had told Esther she was attending an AA meeting on the outskirts of town. She wasn't, of course. A couple of pints down at The Red Hen sounded like a far more appealing option.

When she entered, Gemma was faced with a plump man whose stomach spilt over his belt. A collection of shot glasses beside him, overpowering cologne and a single rose indicated he'd been stood up.

"Mind if I join you?" Gemma asked, slightly hesitant.

"Be my guest," Mick muttered, taking a hefty swig of whiskey on the rocks.

"What are you in for then, partner," Mick snorted, signalling to the barmaid for another round.

"Could ask you the same question."

"A gentlewoman never tells," Mick said, winking.

An hour had passed and without realising it, the conversation hadn't run dry.

"Didn't fancy bringing your wife then?" Mick said.

Gemma choked on her drink, letting out a cackle, "fiancé, actually. How did you know that-?"

"About a minute after meeting you," Mick said, grinning, "nothing gets past me."

Gemma took another swig, the initial burning at the back of her throat, now numb, "Well, with that attention to detail, you ought to become a Detective."

There was a short pause before Mick went into his pocket and pulled out his ID. Stated on it was the title SERGENT MICK PORTER. Underneath, a photograph of him looking both younger and healthier.

Gemma flushed red, putting her glass of merlot to shame.

"Bloody hell, sorry, I didn't-"

"Don't mention it."

"I would *love* to be a Detective you know. Always have if I'm honest. All those shows, *The Bill*, *Midsummer Murders*. They all fascinate me."

"So, what's stopping you?" Mick asked, glaring at Gemma.

Gemma's eyes wondered round the back of the bar and then back down at her drink.

"I suppose life gets in the way. I've always found something to stop me."

Mick slammed his shot glass down theatrically, "now listen here young lady, that is the biggest load of shit anyone has ever spewed. An excuse is what it is."

Gemma sighed, "that's what my fiancé says."

"Well maybe you should bloody well listen to her, she sounds like an intelligent woman."

The more alcohol Gemma consumed, the more broken promises were made between her and Mick. She'd promised him she'd come down to the Station for a meeting and he'd sort of promised her an interview for receptionist in a drunken haze, to get her career ball rolling.

When she got there the next day, things just clicked. Mick was apologetic and poorly disguising the fact he had a hangover. However, despite that, Gemma did her job and she did it well.

After a few months of doing reception work, she decided that she was going to fulfil her potential and become a Detective. With the help of Mick, she undertook her police training. That took her about fourteen weeks, but she didn't care. She enjoyed it. Then, the time came when Mick gave her some experience and she shadowed on the job for a while. With each day, she grew more and more determined. The rest they say is history.

***

Weeks came and went like buses. Gemma had nothing to do but wait for the verdict on the evidence that had been given against Esther. What on earth was the CPS playing at? This was her life. For them, this was just another case, and Gemma understood that, it was just difficult when the shoe was on the other foot.

Due to one of her many hamartia's being impatience, Gemma decided to try and assert some level of control herself. She rang Mick.

"Gem," Mick said, his tone, a silent declaration of despair.

"What do you know? Or not," Gemma fired back.

"Do you want the bad news or the bad news?"

Every possible verdict ran through Gemma's head. Her palms grew clammy and beads of sweat began to form on her forehead.

"Mick don't mess me around. Come on."

There was a heavy sigh on the other end of the phone. The weight of it implying what Gemma had suspected.

"It's the CPS. They've reviewed the evidence we've given against Esther."

"And?"

"I'm sorry to do this Gem, but they've decided not to charge her. The evidence is insufficient."

"Are you having a laugh?" Gemma spat, "The texts were sent from her bloody phone! There's motive written all over it!"

"I know. We're just as frustrated about this as you Gem."

"Oh Mick, not to be rude but you've no idea the week I've had."

A moment of silence naturally broke up the conversation.

"So, what? What other leads have they got?"

"We're both working on it. We've got a few suspects in mind that we're hoping to interview as soon as possible."

Gemma's trembling breath was all that could be heard down the end of the phone.

"So, Esther gets off?"

Mick sighed, "I'm sorry, Gem. If the evidence is deemed insufficient, she's considered an innocent person. They can't let us charge her with the murder of Emma Langley."

The weight of his words pushed against Gemma's chest. She was certain that Esther was involved in this one way or another. She was finally realising all the red flags she'd ignored for years. In hindsight, she should have acted. She should have done her job as a Detective.

"What about prints? On Emma?"

"We found nothing, Gem. Nothing leading back to Esther. The only thing she is guilty of at this point is adultery. The texts clearly indicate that the pair were...involved."

"Esther was trying to get Emma to keep her mouth shut. It's obvious."

"Even if it is Gem, it all comes down to what we can prove in court, and at this moment in time, there's nothing apart from those texts that ties Esther to Emma Langley."

TOBY'S REVENGE

AFTER THE MURDER: THE INVESTIGATION
ESTHER

The energies of previous psychopaths who festered in the very seat she sat in were palpable. She could smell their fear and taste their guilt lingering on the surface of her tongue.

"Esther Quinn," Nigel said, flat and weightless.

"Nige. How are the kids- "

"Officer Smith will be sufficient, thank you," Nigel snapped.

It seemed that Esther's girl next door façade wasn't going to wash with Nigel. He'd built a bond with Gemma. She was his friend as well as his colleague. He wasn't about to jeopardise that relationship for the world. He felt sick to his stomach. He'd let this woman, this criminal slouched in front of him around his kids, his wife. Confronting the possibility that she might be severely dangerous filled him with unimaginable guilt and anger.

Once Esther had received the message from Nigel that he wasn't going to play nice, she shed her skin too and played dirty.

"Alright then, what the fuck do you want?"

Nigel's skin was tight over his knuckles, "why did you kill Emma Langley?"

The tension on Esther's face loosened, along with the certainty of her immunity, her master plan, destabilised.

"How much do you *really* know about her?" Esther asked.

"Well I suppose it would have been easier to just ask her, but unfortunately, she's dead," Nigel said with a crooked smile.

"Not her," Esther said, rolling her eyes, "Gem."

"I know Gemma McCarthy better than you ever could. Than you ever will," Nigel barked.

Esther's eyes narrowed. She let out a dramatic laugh, throwing her head back. Once she'd finished, she stared at Nigel incredulously, "Oh dear, young Nigel. What a fool you are. Gemma never cared about any of you. She couldn't wait to be rid of you all."

"Look, Esther, the only subject I want to discuss is Emma Langley, the woman you murdered? The woman who had her eyes and lips cut off her face? The women who had to be identified by dental records because of the state she was found in," Nigel bellowed, his quivering fingers pointing to the gruesome images of Emma Langley's body.

"She told you about the alcoholism I take it? Or was she too pissed to remember?" Esther said, followed by a false laugh.

"Esther, did you ever have reason to despise Mrs Langley? You were lovers at one point, correct?" Nigel asked, powering on in his attempt to ignore her comments.

Esther looked down and smiled as if reminiscing on a pleasant memory.

"She was a good fuck if that's what you mean."

Nigel looked Esther up and down in utter disgust. He wondered how on earth Gemma could have fallen in love with this woman.

"So, you're confirming that you, Esther Quinn, had a sexual relationship with Emma Langley?" Nigel pressed.

"We were sleeping together for a few years on and off in France. Then, I literally cut her off. She loved me. She wanted to be with me but I wasn't interested. I had other plans. There is nothing else to tell."

"Apart from the fact that you murdered her."

Esther's shoulders raised and she inhaled deeply through her nostrils.

"Look, I don't know what the hell you think you know, but you're wrong. I wouldn't hurt Emma."

"Fine line between love and hate," Nigel paused, "did one override the other, Esther? Maybe it was the fact that she threatened to ruin the life Gemma had given to you and tell her what her faithful fiancé had been up to?"

Leaning forward, Nigel switched off the recorder and stared at Esther square in the face. The proximity was close enough that he could feel smell Esther's breath. Cheap coffee and stale cigarettes.

"Now, I'm going to tell you something off record and I hope you're listening. I am something of a connoisseur when it comes to your kind. No matter how hard you try to run, we'll always be right behind you, fighting even harder to make sure your evil soul never encounters any other citizen of Oakley Green again."

Esther gulped.

Nigel believed that his Jason Statham performance had succeeded in poking holes through her act. Witness to the exposure of her true colours, he had faith that she would crack.

He flicked the switch and proceeded with the interview.

"Well if you didn't do it, who did you get to do it for you?" Nigel asked, skimming through the files of images taken from the crime scene.

Esther folded her arms, leaned back in and started up at the ceiling.

"Perhaps these images will jog your memory," Nigel said, pushing the files forward.

The further he pushed them; the further Esther moved away.

"How the fuck is this relevant? Shouldn't you be doing your job and finding the evil bastard that did it?"

Nigel's eyebrows elevated, along with his temper.

"Look at the images," he snapped.

Esther struggled to look for more than a couple of seconds before her eyes flickered away.

"I already told you, I didn't do it!" She yelled, slamming both hands onto the table.

"But you're going to conceal the fact that you know who did, and for what?"

"I'd like to be released now. You've no concrete evidence. You can't charge me."

Nigel laughed, "Oh, but we will, don't you worry. We've got the texts and we've got the images. It's just a matter of time before the truth comes out. The person you've paid to do your dirty work will soon come to light and there will be nothing you can do about it."

Gemma had been staying at a hotel for a few weeks since Esther had been released. She couldn't stand the thought of going back home. The memories of what they had would be far too painful to stomach, even if she was publicly declared innocent.

Gemma knew the truth, deep in her gut. She wanted to miss Esther but stopped herself at the thought of her holding a knife in her hand and being capable of all the things that Emma Langley had done to her.

That was the thing, too. She wanted to be angry at Emma. She wanted so desperately to have given her a good slap, but she figured Emma had experienced enough brutality, leading to a slow and painful death. The thought of hating her felt wrong but she couldn't stifle the wave of it, oozing out like blood that wouldn't clot.

Gemma's phone rang. It was Mick.

"Morning, lazy bones."

"Eh? Gemma said, checking the time. 10:30. *Shit.*

"Ah, Mick. I'm sorry. I was up all night, just thinking, you know. I'm sorry."

"Eh, never mind. Not every day that your fiancé is arrested on suspicion of murder, is it?"

"Has Esther been staying at the house?"

"Yes, and if it makes you feel better, we've got the front and back surrounded by officers. We've still got her phone. The team are trying to find anything we might have missed."

"And you'll let me know? When you find something?"

"Of course, Gem, but please tell me you'll get out of that Hotel room? At least for an hour."

"Maybe, yeah."

"Promise me."

It had felt like a year since Gemma had been back to work. She couldn't really envisage what it would be like after such horrendous circumstances, apart from extremely intense and awkward. *What a weak relationship they must have had, for her not to know her own fiancé was a murderer,* Gemma could hear them all saying. Or, *they weren't even married… what a poor excuse for a marriage it would have been, do you think she knew that her fiancé was a psychopath? Could she sense it somehow?*

Anyway, she'd been through worse than this and she knew it. At some point, she needed to get on with her life again, but it was so bloody difficult.

Fiancé not charged for a murder that she *did* commit but *didn't* in the eyes of the CPS. No more wedding planning of any kind. No future with the woman she thought she loved. The potential loss of her job if constant moping continued. Not only that, but Gemma hadn't heard from Mick or Nigel about any other potential leads on the case.

Despite Gemma being almost certain that Esther was nothing more than a lying, cheating bitch who murdered her ex, it was going to take more than some texts to prove that she had carried out this unspeakable crime.

People had to believe Gemma about Esther's evil capabilities, which was strange for her to understand since she had barely come to terms with it herself. But no matter how long it took, she was going to solve this case. She was going to put this nightmare to bed and try to salvage what was left of her life. All she needed to do was just be smart like she usually was. She needed evidence. Undeniable, old-fashioned, cold, hard evidence.

Once the upset had gradually subsided, anger was all that remained, like a hideous scar.

It was almost like something had shoved her back into reality. She was a Detective. She was an excellent Detective. She needed to solve this case, and not just for her sake. Perhaps, she thought, it was her Mother looking down on her and giving her a slap in the face, telling her to grow up and get on with things. But then, she laughed it off, cringing at herself for even slightly convincing herself that she was the spiritual type. She was anything but.

But she was no use to anyone stuck in bed all day, festering in her own filth, bags under her eyes deeper than her pain. She felt like one of those Bridget Jones types. Sat on the sofa, bawling, stuffing her face with junk food, engulfed by copious amounts of scrunched up balls of tissues, scattered across her mattress like poppies in a field.

She knew what she had to do. She had to solve this case and she had to do it fast. She wasn't trying to undermine the work of Mick and Nigel, or the rest of her colleagues, but somewhere inside herself, she knew she had what it took to solve this case. Maybe it was the fire inside her, the rage that had been created following these tragic events. Maybe it was just her, something she couldn't answer for. Anyhow, she could feel it there and it was now that she had to act. It was time to follow her instincts like she should have done all along.

"Mick?"

"Gem, everything alright? Apart from the obvious?" Mick's gravelly voice greeted Gemma like an old friend.

"Mick, I'm fine. I'd like to come back to work. I'd like to continue with the case if you'll have me?"

There was a small groan on the other end of the phone.

"Oh, Gem. I wouldn't want to throw you back into this mess when you're already dealing with so much. My only worry is that you'll relapse because of the pressure."

"Mick. Can I ask you a question?"

"Anything."

"When you trained me, did I ever back down? Did I ever turn down a case despite how hard it was?"

"No, Gemma, you didn't," Mick said, a smile in his voice.

"So, what makes you think I'm going to back down now? After I've lost everything?"

"Very well, Gem. What is it you're thinking?"

"I'm glad you asked. I want to interview Toby again. I feel like he has more to say to me than he let on the other day."

"Like what? You think it's something serious?"

"I'm not sure, but I have a feeling. I feel like he knows something. Like he's guarding a secret for someone."

He looked different the next time around. His hair wasn't as impeccably positioned as is usually was when Gemma met with him. He didn't look all put together. Perhaps the framework he'd believed to be so secure had faltered. Perhaps, this time, he would tell Gemma what he knew. What he'd known all along. She couldn't quite put her finger on it, but Gemma had always had a sixth sense with these kinds of things. He was hiding something and she was going to get to the bottom of it.

"We meet again, Toby."

"We do, *Gemma*. Are we recovering well? I heard you've been through quite a tragedy these past few weeks?"

He held her gaze far longer this time, not blinking once.

"And who might you have heard that from?"

Toby didn't respond. He smirked, played with his hands. Another crack in his framework.

"I suppose you're just doing your job, Gemma, although, I'm quite intrigued, as I've heard that you've found your killer. And so, surely you require my assistance no more?"

Little shit. He's starting to really piss me off, the little voice in Gemma's head whispered to her again. But she couldn't indulge. It was imperative she remained calm and collected. Especially in the presence of Toby. If he could sense a flicker of anxiety or vulnerability, it would all be off. She'd lose the thread she was using to string him along.

"Well, unfortunately, Toby, these investigations are complicated, such as life. You must understand? A smart young man like yourself ought to know that?"

"I may have some understanding, yes."

Gemma felt the heat rising inside her, all the way to her head. This little bastard was toying with her. How did he know she'd been through a tragedy anyway?

"Toby, do you remember when you asked me if I liked other women in our first interview together?"

Toby smirked, "I suppose. Why is that relevant?"

Gemma took out a thumbnail picture of Esther from her purse. She slapped it on the table in front of Toby and watched as his cheeks were stained red. Silence hung in the air between them, oppressive and impatient.

"Recognise this woman?" Gemma probed.

Toby's face transformed. He went from being a vulnerable little boy, to acting like an arrogant, self-righteous brat.

"I've never seen that woman in my life," he said, arms folded, chest pushed out, a blank expression wiped across his face.

Gemma proceeded, pressing her lips together so tightly that her teeth almost cut through to the skin. She was reaching her limit. If he wasn't going to give the information up easily, she'd have to push a little harder.

"Listen, Toby, I'm not pissing about here- "

"To tell you the truth, Detective, I may have seen her a few months ago, before Mrs Langley's murder," Toby interrupted. "it was break time. I was *obviously* in Detention for *obviously*, nothing. From the class I was caged in, I could see right out to the car park. Mrs Langley was packing our English papers into her shitty car, along with our textbooks. From the corner of my eye, I remember spotting a rather attractive woman. Brown hair, slim, elegantly dressed."

Gemma's stomach dropped at the familiarity and of Toby's description.

"And, what happened? Did they seem familiar with one another?"

"Oh yes, Detective, very much so," Toby said, grinning to himself like it was his own private joke.

"Did they seem friendly?"

"Very friendly indeed. The woman ran behind Mrs Langley in what looked like an attempt to scare her in a jovial way. Mrs Langley turned around, the pair kissed and got into her car. You could tell that it was secretive. Mrs Langley seemed worried that someone might catch her. After all, she was a married woman."

"And was this the only time that you'd seen them together?"

"As I said, I'm not entirely sure if it was this woman who I saw, fondling with Mrs Langley."

Gemma's stomach tightened.

"Did you ever have any contact with the woman you saw?"

"We spoke once or twice, usually when she was waiting outside for Mrs Langley to finish her marking. I used to stay late to catch up on work some nights. Even so, I didn't analyse her face in a lot of depth."

"Did she say who she was? Why she was there?"

"She did give her name, but, it's such a pity, Gemma. It seems to have slipped my memory."

Little bastard, the little voice hissed.

"Look, I'm going to be completely honest with you and I need you to reciprocate."

"Anything to help the case, Detective."

"You wouldn't lie, would you Toby?"

His face twisted in contemplation at the question, whether or not he could truly commit to what Gemma was asking. In her gut, Gemma was uncertain whether to put her trust in him for information. After all, he was a young boy, yet he seemed so much older. She had to keep reminding herself of that. He wasn't an adult. He was a child.

"Never, Detective," Toby said, grinning deceitfully.

"Toby, I'm sure that my fiancé, this woman in the photograph, Esther, murdered Mrs Langley. I'm sorry if that comes as a shock to you. But I'm positive. All I need you to do is tell me everything you know about her, if the woman you saw was the same woman in the photograph. We need to build a strong case against her so that Mrs Langley and her family receive justice. I'm sure that's what you want too, isn't it Toby?"

"I, I don't know Detective. I don't want to get too involved in the case."

Gemma sniggered, "Oh, Toby. You already are."

After almost an hour of questioning, Gemma left the school, staring back at Toby as she did. He looked straight through her with his glistening pearlescent pools for eyes.

TOBY'S REVENGE

He'd waved goodbye to her reluctantly. She'd told him to make sure he contacted her whenever he remembered anything about what he'd seen, anything suspicious. He assured her he would, though with sarcasm.

When Gemma made her way back to the Station, Nigel was at the Reception, waiting. He looked relieved at her arrival. Something in him lit up. Each feature on his face appeared more alert.

He mouthed her name through the smudged windows and pointed towards the conference room.

Gemma sauntered in with caution. Nigel and Mick both sat, staring up at her knowingly. Gemma opened her mouth ready to speak, but just as she did, Nigel shot up, nearly knocking a hot mug of coffee over Mick's lap.

"We got a call from the lab last night."

Gemma's pulse thumped in her ears, not stopping until Nigel went to speak again.

"We didn't want to tell you until you were back, but we've had an update on the case. The SOCO extracted some evidence from Emma Langley's body. It's hair, and some fibres from what they suspect to be a coat or jacket. The fibers are bright red, they're a cotton material. "

"And, they found a match? That's enough to send Esther down."

Nigel darted Mick a look. Mick's face dropped.

"What is it? What are we waiting for?" Gemma asked, desperation in her voice.

"I'm sorry, Gem. The DNA they found didn't match with Esther's profile. Esther isn't our killer."

The sour bitter taste of bile slid up to the back of Gemma's throat. She felt her knees giving way.

"But it has to be her? The texts, she- "

"We're as shocked as you are, Gem. But, in all honesty, the texts don't prove Esther was at the scene of the crime, only that she had threatened Emma Langley prior to her death."

Gemma's tongue stuck to the roof of her mouth, the moisture of it drying up.

"So, if it wasn't Esther, then... who was it?"

"The DNA evidence correlated instantly with some DNA we have on the National Database. The evidence gathered belongs to that of a Mr Toby Devourt."

"No, no," Gemma protested, grabbing a seat as if her life depended on it. All of a sudden, the room felt like it was spinning. The words Nigel had said, spinning with it, round and round in her head, unable to be paused, stuck on repeat.

"You were right, Gem. About the boy. There was something he was hiding," Mick said, kneeling down to hold Gemma's hand that was shaking like a leaf in a storm.

"Wha- what do we do now?" Gemma managed through clenched teeth.

"We've got a warrant. We'll make our way to the Devourt residence soon."

TOBY'S REVENGE

"Mick, are you sure? You're certain?"

"DNA never lies, Gem."

BEFORE THE MURDER

ESTHER

(2) MISSED CALLS – MUM X

How she wished it was her mum. But it was *her*. She'd been constantly texting Esther all day, pleading her to answer her calls.

An hour had passed. Emma had called again, but Esther hadn't picked up. She thought perhaps she'd give up and realise that Esther wasn't interested in what she had to say. But of course, she didn't.

"What do you want?" Esther answered.

On the other end of the phone, Emma's breathing was sombre, each breath like a sigh.

"Em? What do you want from me?"

"Esther, we don't have to do this. We can be together, just me and you. We can drive wherever we want, tonight? Please say you'll come with me?"

"Are you delusional? Of course, I'm not coming with you. What about my life here? I've got it good here. I have an amazing house, a stable job, Gemma."

"But we're- "

"Don't even say it, Em. We're not in love, okay? We were lucky enough to see each other again and have some fun together, but that was it. It's time we both moved on, don't you think?"

"Moved on?"

Esther could feel Emma's anger through the phone. She was going to do something stupid.

"I'm sorry Esther, but you're not thinking straight," Emma said, "if you're not going to come to your senses and tell Gemma about us, then I will."

"Emma, listen to me," Esther said calmly, trying not to create get Emma riled up further, "Gemma will not know about us. If you tell her, I will never speak to you again. Is that what you want?"

"Too late, Esther. It's either her or me. You have one more day to decide. After that, whatever happens, will happen."

"Emma, you can't do this. You will not do this," Esther ordered through clenched teeth.

For a moment, Esther didn't get a response. Then, the call cut off with a dull thud.

"Emma?"

BEFORE THE MURDER

TOBY

It was that afternoon, Toby noticed Mrs Langley acting crazier than she usually did. She seemed to be riding the neurotic wave of one of her episodes.

Toby watched her as she spoke to the class in an over-enthusiastic, high pitched voice. She'd never usually behaved this way. She'd always appeared to be defeated in the afternoon. Hanging her head over the desk, marking papers sloppily whilst the class were forced to read a chapter of *The Great Gatsby* and analyse the symbolism of the green light.

He tried to figure out where she'd got this new wave of energy from. Had she taken some kind of pill? Had she done some drugs in the staff toilets? *It wouldn't be the first time,* Toby thought as he was reminded of the time Mr Wilson, the science teacher got arrested for snorting coke off one of the student's textbooks last year.

When the bell rang and the class was dismissed, Toby stayed behind, pretending to write the last part of his answer.

"Toby, the bell has spoken, it's time to go now," Emma said, pointing to the classroom door.

"Oh, I know Mrs Langley, it's just Fitzgerald's work is simply far too riveting to walk away from, wouldn't you agree?"

Emma sighed, leant back in her chair and stared at Toby with utter disdain.

"What is it about you, Toby? Trouble at home? Mum not paying you enough attention? Dad being a knob?"

Toby's fists clenched at the mentioning of his father.

"Oh, sorry, did I hit a nerve? Did I offend you?" Emma said, smirking and looking back down at her papers.

TOBY'S REVENGE

Toby's rage continued to grow. *How dare she.*

"You know nothing about my father. He'd be the only person to put you in your place."

"Oh, is that right? Well, bring him in! What a great idea. I'll tell him what a little shit you've been this year and perhaps he'll put you in your place, Toby."

"I can't bring him in, he's dead."

Emma looked up and pulled a sad face, "Oh dear, what a shame," she said, gathering her stuff and making her way to the door, "Oh, when you're finished with that, close the door behind you. I'll know it was you if it hasn't been locked."

How dare she. She'll get what's coming to her. No one insults my father's memory like that.

BEFORE THE MURDER

ESTHER

Shit. Part of Esther knew she was in trouble. She knew in her gut that Emma was going to say something. She was going to go to Gemma and tell her everything, and then she'd lose everything.

She tried getting hold of Emma but each time, the call went straight to voicemail.

"Look, Em, it's Esther. We need to talk about this, properly. We can talk about us but don't tell Gemma. I'll tell her, in my own time," Esther said, leaving the voicemail.

She had to act now. What if Emma had already gone to Gemma? What if Gemma knew and was already planning to kick Esther out?

TOBY'S REVENGE

Esther jumped in the car in a panic. She made her way to the school to see if she had a chance of catching Emma. She hoped she had one more chance to prevent her from saying anything.

BEFORE THE MURDER

TOBY

Just as he was putting his bag on, Toby noticed the same women he'd seen with Mrs Langley when he was in detention. She seemed to be rushing, in some sort of panic. But the school was closing now? What could she possibly be doing here at this time, and what did she want?

He rushed out to see what was wrong with her.

"Excuse me, Miss? Are you alright?"

Esther ran her hands through her hair and stopped as if she was preparing to pull it all out.

"I'm sorry, young man. I'm just looking for my friend, I'll come back later."

"Mrs Langley? You're looking for her, aren't you?"

Esther froze. She turned to face him.

"How do you know that? What has she said?"

"Oh, no she hasn't uttered a word. Actually, I saw you both by her car that day. You kissed her."

Esther's cheeks flushed red. She took a deep breath and sat on the floor of the car park, her head in her hands.

Toby looked around to see if anyone was watching them. There was no one around. He walked up to Esther and sat with her.

"Are you okay? Has she done something to upset you?"

Esther took her head out from her hands and looked up at Toby, her face sweaty and covered in tears.

"She, she's going to ruin my life. She's going to tell my fiancé that we were having an affair and I don't know how to stop it."

"Oh, I thought as much. Quite a bitch isn't she," Toby said, checking his phone.

"You, you don't like her?"

"I hope I'm not offending you too much, but as it goes, no I don't. Actually, I hate her."

A stunned expression spread across Esther's face. Toby had wondered if he'd probably gone too far.

"You're that kid that she's always going on about. Tony, is it? You give her shit all the time."

Toby frowned.

"Toby, actually. And, I'd like to think that she is the one who gives me shit actually. She's a miserable woman who cheats on her husband and only cares about herself. Sometimes I think she'd be better off- "

"Dead?"

BEFORE THE MURDER

ESTHER

She knew it sounded evil, but she couldn't think of any other way to ensure that Emma would be out of her life for good. If she was still alive, she would still be out there and she would still always have the chance to come back and ruin things for Esther. The risk couldn't be taken. Esther had to act, and quickly.

"My name's Esther, Esther Quinn," Esther said, holding out her hand to Toby.

He shook it.

"Toby, Toby Devourt."

They both smiled awkwardly.

"Listen, Toby, I know this might sound extremely insane, but-"

"You want me to help get rid of Mrs. Langley?"

"Well, I... yes."

"Count me in."

Esther's heart started racing. She was actually going to go through with this. Emma would be gone and she'd never see her again. Part of her was upset, but the other part of her was relieved. She wouldn't have to keep constantly looking over her shoulder, wondering whether today would be the day that her life got taken away from her. She had to do this. There was no other way.

"It's just, I'm not a killer, I- "

"Please, Esther. Leave it to me. I will take care of it. All you need to do is get me some tools and get Mrs Langley to meet you here at the school in an hour. Tell her you need to talk about your relationship and that it's urgent. Tell her to meet in her classroom."

"But what if she gets caught coming back into school?"

"If she gets caught, she could say she forgot something? Some books maybe? She's a teacher."

Toby was building up an image in Esther's mind. An image of how easy this could be. It would all be over in a few seconds. She'd lure Emma back to the classroom; Toby would come out and kill her. That way, she wasn't really guilty, was she?"

"Okay, I'll call her."

"No, wait," Toby said, snatching her phone, "Tools, first. I need something to hit her with."

"Oh, yeah sure," Esther said, going into the boot of her car, her hands shaking. She found a large hammer and a box cutter.

She held them up for Toby's approval.

He nodded, gesturing her to pass them over.

"It will be quick, won't it? She'll die instantly, almost like it was an accident and she just hit her head?" Esther asked desperately.

Toby grinned.

"Just like an accident. A terrible accident."

BEFORE THE MURDER

EMMA

Emma was driving home on the bumpy roads in this town that she was beginning to despise. Couldn't they fork out and pay for some new roads to be built?

Anyway, the roads were the least of her worries. She had to get Esther back. She had to make her realise that them breaking up was a huge mistake. Just as she was thinking of calling her, Esther sent her a text. She pressed down on the breaks and swerved to the side of the road, turning her hazard lights on.

Hey Em, it's me. I've been thinking about what you said. We do have something special. Meet me at the school. We can go into your classroom and talk about this? Love Est. X

Finally, Esther had realised that it was Emma she was meant to be with. All she needed to do was just listen to her heart and she'd find the answer.

Emma went to her contacts and called Esther.

"Hey, Em," Esther answered immediately, her voice sounding chirper.

"Oh my God, Esther. I love you. I can't believe it took you so long to realise."

"I know, my love. I'm so sorry, I really do love you. Please, just meet me at the school, no one is around."

"Are you sure? Maybe we should meet somewhere else? A little more private?"

"No," Esther snapped, "I'm already here."

"Oh... okay. I'll just turn around."

"Yes, do that. Please hurry, I can't wait to see you."

BEFORE THE MURDER

EMMA

Emma felt peculiar, driving into her place of work when it was 6: 00.pm. It was a miserable evening, oppressive and solemn, like something from a Gothic tale.

When she'd parked her car, Emma scanned the area, looking for any sign of Esther. She wasn't there.

"Esther?" Emma called, walking nearer to the entrance of the school to see if she was waiting there. And there she was, sobbing, leaning by the door.

"Em!" she shouted, running into Emma's arms and hugging her tightly.

"Esther, how long have you been waiting here?" Emma asked, running Esther's arms and kissing her on the forehead.

"Oh, not too long, although it would be nice to go inside?"

"Oh, of course," Emma said, fumbling around in her pocket for the keys.

BEFORE THE MURDER

TOBY

Once Esther had handed over the tools, Toby was set. He was ecstatic, like an infant who had been given some shiny new toys to play with.

He told Esther to hide near the door and wait for Emma's arrival. With the hammer, Toby had managed to smash through the window of the classroom and get inside without an alarm going off.

They probably didn't work anyway, Toby thought, *they've got better things to spend their money on.*

After brushing himself off, Toby made his way over to Mrs Langley's desk. He analysed it for a moment, taking in the opportunity he'd been given to really teach her a lesson.

TOBY'S REVENGE

It would be the last time she stood behind that desk and made him feel small in front of the class.

He was getting his revenge, and it tasted sweet.

He laid tools out. First, the hammer. Second, the box cutter.

He twisted his head to the side in contemplation at the box cutter. The blade was so precise. It would mean that whenever he'd make a cut, the line would be far too perfect. She would die quickly and without a struggle. This just wouldn't do.

He eyes darted to the corner of the classroom where Mrs Langley kept the scissors for them to use. Typically, these would be used to cutting out paper shapes or worksheets and sticking them to posters and exercise books. But Toby had other ideas. He'd found a new purpose for them. And Mrs Langley would find out exactly what that was.

BEFORE THE MURDER

ESTHER

It was really happening. All of a sudden, Esther felt a lump in her throat when she saw how elated Emma had been when she saw her. She was truly content. That was about to be taken away from her by someone she thought she could trust. For a moment Esther dwelled on the thought, do you ever really know someone?

They were approaching Emma's classroom now and everything seemed surreal. It was like she was an actress, playing the part of a murder. The reality of the situation failed to surface. All the while though, to stop the guilt from seeping in, she thought of her life with Gemma. She thought of how privileged she was and about how that meant more to her really than Emma did. Part of her was apologetic, but the other part knew this was the only solution.

Emma jingled her keys to find the right one. When she did, she poked it through. It slid in with no trouble. Then, with a firm shove, the door was open.

They were in. They were finally in.

Esther walked in first and tried to spot Toby. She couldn't see him, but she saw a plastic bag in the corner with his shoes thrown in. He was there too.

"So, what did you want to talk about? How about we start with where we're going to go when we pack up? Have you even packed?"

Esther froze to the spot. Her heart was thumping against her chest and breathing became a strenuous ordeal.

"Emma- "

TOBY'S REVENGE

Just as she went to speak, Toby burst out from behind the bookshelf with the hammer Esther had given him. He sped towards Emma without a second thought, pushed her onto the floor and struck her to the back of the head at least six times. The blows were firm. Emma screamed. She tried to cover her face, but Toby was too strong. The final blow killed her. Blood splattered in every direction. Pieces of gooey brain matter stuck to the hammer.

Esther was paralysed. She stood, focused on Toby who seemed to be in a world of his own. She'd never seen someone so in awe.

"that'll teach you, Mrs Langley," Toby whispered in Emma's battered ear.

In a final insult, Toby took out a pair of classroom scissors from his pocket. He stood back and admired his work. Then, he bent down and cut off Emma's lips, throwing them to the side when he had finished like they were pieces of rubbish. He moved onto her eyelids, slicing them off unevenly and throwing them too.

"I don't suppose you'll want to stay for the rest, will you?" Toby asked Esther who had no colour in her face. She was shaking.

All of a sudden, she was sick, all over Emma's desk.

"I thought that might happen," Toby said, wiping the sweat off his brow.

BEFORE THE MURDER

TOBY

It was difficult. Cutting her eyelids off was seemingly harder than Toby had imagined. The skin was extremely thin and the fatty tissue around the eye kept getting in the way. Her lips were easy enough, though. Very plump, very soft, delicate skin on her lips.

He wondered how many people had kissed with those lips? Probably thousands, knowing her.

"I gave you a warning. Maybe not verbally, but you definitely knew what I meant. This is what happens when you don't listen," Toby said, looking down at Mrs Langley's body.

Poor Esther, she won't be able to clean all this up. It will have to be me.

TOBY'S REVENGE

But he wasn't finished yet. The fun had only just started.

BEFORE THE MURDER

ESTHER

"What are w-we going to do with her?"

"Well, we are not going to do anything. I will sort this out, Esther. Don't worry. You asked me to help you and that's what I've done."

Esther was still shaking, unable to vocalise her emotions. Extreme regret sat in the pit of her stomach like a large stone, weighing her down.

"Go, leave. You don't want to get caught here, do you?" Toby barked.

Esther shook her head profusely, grabbing her bag and scurrying out to her car.

TOBY'S REVENGE

Once she put her key in and started the engine, everything that had happened came crashing down on her. She screamed and cried in her car for hours before leaving the car park. The noise of Toby bashing Emma's skull. The smell of the classroom, the look in Emma's eyes. It was all coming back to her in unforgiving waves. *Is this what Macbeth felt like?* She wondered. *Would the guilt ever wash away or would it be absorbed into her skin for eternity?*

AFTER THE MURDER

TOBY

Once Esther had gone, Toby was alone with Mrs Langley.

He studied her face for hours. He couldn't believe he had the last laugh. It pleased him, though. He had defended his father's honour and he had defended the Devourt name. his father would be proud of him.

He had done what was asked of him, but now, it was time to clean up this mess.

AFTER THE MURDER: THE INVESTIGATION

GEMMA

It was nothing otherworldly, as Gemma had imagined. Perhaps a marble staircase, elaborate garden decorations and thousands of exotic flowers suffocating the front entrance of the mansion? But no, underwhelmingly, Toby's home was average. It was a house that any other family might live in.

Gemma watched on as Mick, almost out of breath, traipsed his way through the front garden and up to the door, weeds spilling onto the concrete, threatening to lasso us up. Nigel followed right behind. Gemma was directly behind him.

How could this be happening? She thought, *why would he want to do this? How could he, a fourteen-year-old boy, possibly want to be involved?*

When they arrived at the front door, Mick knocked loudly, twice. There was no answer for a few minutes, so he tried again. Then, what seemed to be Toby's mother, hobbled to the door with a cigarette in her arthritic hand, burning right down to the lettering, ash falling like snow onto the unwashed flooring.

"What do you lot want?"

"Hello, Mrs Devourt?"

"This is she," She croaked, taking another desperate drag of her cigarette.

"We're incredibly sorry to bother you like this, Mrs Devourt. But unfortunately, your son, Toby's DNA has been identified at a murder scene. We have a search warrant."

Her beady eyes darted from each one of us.

"Toby! You've got visitors," She called up the stairs, leaving the front door ajar and gesturing us to come in.

Gemma was speechless to find no sign of shock or worry on Mrs Devourt's face. It was like she'd been through this before. Then, Gemma thought back to the story of Toby's father, Greg. Perhaps, being married to him would have meant you were familiar with the police.

Toby skipped down the stairs, a merry grin on his face. He stared directly at Gemma.

"Ah, Gemma. I was wondering how long it would be until you turned up here. You've taken your time; I'll tell you that for nothing."

Gemma was silent. Every muscle clenched up.

"Toby, we've got a search warrant, we'll be going up to your room now. You need to stay here," Mick said, analysing Toby's face for a lot longer than was normally expected, "You have his eyes," Mick said, followed by a shudder.

Mick and Nigel darted upstairs, leaving Gemma and Toby together in the hallway.

"Toby. You need to tell me; did Esther ask you to do this?"

Toby grinned, "What is it I'm supposed to say? Oh, yes, no comment."

Gemma could feel herself losing it. Her reigns on her rage were loosening. She was failing to get a grip on them.

"Why are you protecting her?"

"Some people need protecting, Gemma. Isn't that the reason you became a Detective?"

"You mark my words, Toby, I'll find out exactly what you did. You and her. You'll both go down for a very, very long time," Gemma hissed.

"Find!" Mick bellowed from the top of the stairs, holding up a red school jumper, spatters of dried blood sprinkled along the edges like an Alexander McQueen piece.

Toby's face dropped, along with the rest of his body.

"You hid it well, lad, I'll give you that," Mick said, looking at Toby, then at Mrs Devourt, waving the jumper around.

"Toby Devourt, you're under arrest on the suspicion of murdering Mrs Emma Langley.

"You do not have to say anything. But it may harm your defence if you do not mention when questioned something which you later rely on in court. Anything you do say may be given in evidence," Nigel said with a smug grin on his face, cuffing Toby's wrists.

There was an air of sadness and despair when the team noticed Toby's wrists were too small for the cuffs. They'd slid right out. They'd have to escort him to the car by taking his arms instead. One arm each.

Mrs Devourt seemed to have that expression of expectancy on her face. It was as if she had somehow predicted this day.

When Toby was leaving, she turned to look at him.

"Goodbye, son."

TOBY'S REVENGE

AFTER THE MURDER: THE INVESTIGATION

GEMMA

Questioning Toby had to be the most surreal experience of Gemma's career. He sat there, like the schoolboy he was, slumped in the chair opposite her.

"Do you want a drink, Toby? Water, tea?" Gemma asked, as if saying the words were causing her physical pain. Toby didn't respond.

"So, Toby, we're going to ask you a few questions regarding the murder of Mrs Emma Langley, your English teacher."

Toby rolled his eyes and yawned.

TOBY'S REVENGE

"Did you, Toby Devourt, murder Mrs Emma Langley of Oakley Green?"

Toby's Lawyer whispered something into his ear. Toby then nodded, looked at Gemma and answered, "No comment."

"Toby, we have obtained DNA evidence which places you at the scene of the crime. Is there anything you want to say about this? Any objection?"

"No comment," Toby said, watching Gemma like a hawk.

Every time her was questioned, Toby gave the same reply, providing no further information.

"What the hell did you do to her?" Gemma asked, swallowing hard, trying to sooth the lump in her throat.

Toby remained still and lifeless.

"She helped you, didn't she? She helped you get rid of Emma and you were willing to kill her, for what?"

"I think my client has had enough," Toby's Social Worker interjected.

"I don't give a shit," Gemma said, continuing to stare at Toby.

"Did you enjoy it? Cutting off her lips, watching the blood ooze out? You're a sick little boy. You need help."

"I'm sorry, but my client does not need to hear this. If there are no further questions, we need to stop," Toby's Social bellowed, his double chin swinging like a Turkey's, wrinkly and red.

"Toby Devourt, you will be charged with the murder of Emma Langley. You will be kept in custody at a local authority accommodation until your hearing. One of the guards will escort you there immediately."

"No wonder Esther cheated on you," Toby said, "you're nothing more than a bad Detective who couldn't solve a case."

Gemma felt like she'd been punched in the chest.

"Guard," Gemma called, her eyes not leaving Toby's until he left the room.

When he'd gone, Gemma punched the table, slitting the skin across her knuckle. No one had ever gotten under her skin as Toby had. Not even Esther.

AFTER THE MURDER: THE INVESTIGATION: ESTHER'S CONFESSION

When Esther walked into the Station the following day, her cheeks were soaked with her tears.

Gemma walked out of the interview room after dealing with Toby. She froze at the sight of Esther, her body trembling.

"Guard!" She shouted.

Esther waved her arms and got down on her knees.

"Please, I'm here to confess, I promise," Esther pleaded.

Mick pulled Gemma to one side, trying to calm her down.

"Don't worry, Gem, I've got this," He reassured her, "You can watch from the back room if you want."

"Too right," Gemma snapped, "there's no way I'm missing this."

Mick took Esther's arm and escorted her into the interview room after she'd been patted down by the guards.

She sat in the chair, wilting like a dead flower that had once flourished.

"Esther Quinn, I'm Sergeant Mick Porter. You've come in today to confess to the assisted murder of Mrs Emma Langley of Oakley Green, correct?"

Esther looked up at the camera, "Yes," she managed, sobbing.

"Would you like to tell us what happened, in your own words."

Esther looked at the camera every time she spoke as if somehow, she was talking directly to Gemma. It was like she was apologising.

"Em, Emma wanted us to run away together. But I told her that I loved Gemma. I told her I wanted to stay here. She wasn't having any of it."

"And so, you thought murdering her would be a good idea?" Mick asked.

Esther began to cry, taking a sip of her water. The plastic cup shaking, causing water to spill all over the table.

"Oh, I'm s-sorry," she said, trying to wipe it up with the sleeves of her jacket.

Gemma was reminded of Esther's sweetness. It was hard, to watch someone you once loved, sitting there in pain, struggling, a chrysalis of their former selves. But the fact still remained. Esther had assisted a murder. She could never escape that.

"It's fine, Esther. Please, explain what happened when you saw Emma," Mick continued, not paying any attention to the puddle of water creeping gradually his way.

"Well, I didn't want her to tell Gemma. I didn't want her to tell Gemma that we had slept together and that we were seeing each other. I wanted her to stop. I needed her to- "

"Please, Esther, take your time," Mick interrupted.

Gemma watched from the back room, biting her nails down to the skin.

"I went to Le Petit Oak to try and stop her. I thought she was on her way to my house, to tell Gemma. I panicked. When I got there, it was too late. Her car was gone and Le Petit Oak was shut. That's when I saw Toby," Esther said, her voice growing colder.

"And when you saw Toby, what happened then?"

"I was desperate. He was there, and he spoke to me about Emma. He expressed his hatred for her and in that moment, I felt like we were sort of connected. One the same wavelength, almost. I don't know what was going through my mind, but he offered a sort of solution to the problem."

"What did he say?"

"He said sometimes he thought she'd be better off-"Esther hesitated, tears forming in her eyes.

"She'd be better off what?"

"Well, actually it was me who said it, but he was about to say it. I finished his sentence."

Gemma stared in shock at the screen. *Could it really be her fiancé, Esther Quinn, agreeing to a murder? Who had she been in love with all these years? It felt like everything she had known was slipping through her fingers like water.*

"I agreed to it in a moment of weakness and I shouldn't have. If I knew how it would make me feel, how it makes me feel... I would do anything to go back in time. I would do anything to make things right," Esther said, burying her head in her hands, crying hysterically.

"Did you see Toby kill Emma?"

"Yes. It was awful. I haven't been able to sleep. I was scared. I'm so sorry," Esther said, pouring herself onto the table, completely inconsolable.

Mick concluded the interview and turned the recorder off.

Gemma's heart broke for the second time that day. But she knew in that moment, that no matter how many times her heart was broken, it would repair itself eventually.

She didn't attend the trial, but she heard from people in the local area that Esther received a minimum of eighteen years behind bars for assisting the murder of Emma Langley. She'd heard on the radio that Toby Devourt was to serve the minimum sentence in a correctional rehabilitation facility due to his age.

It made Gemma feel uneasy, to know that one day, Toby might get out. Her faith in the system was faltered at the possibility of Toby being let out due to him being 'rehabilitated' whatever that was supposed to mean.

Overall, she had loved and she had lost. There was one thing for sure that Gemma knew. You never really know someone.

AFTER THE INVESTIGATION

GEMMA

Three months had passed by. Gemma was coping as well as she could. She moved onto other cases and went dating, but Emma Langley's case was like chewing gum. It stuck, tangled in her mind whenever she tried to erase it for even a second.

One day, she hoped it would fade. Along with the memories she kept stored in the back of her mind. Memories of Esther. But for now, it remained an uphill battle and she was going to be late for work.

As she made her way over to her wardrobe where her blazer hung, Gemma heard the flap of her door.

She ran downstairs to see what had been posted. Just beneath, there was a letter addressed to her.

But she'd moved house and hadn't told anyone her new address?

She flipped it round and opened it.

The card was blank. No design on the front. It was bland and non-descript.

Gemma opened it up.

She could feel her heart hammering against her chest. Her breathing slowed.

There. In Bold.

You didn't think you'd get rid of me that easily, did you?

See you around, Gemma.

All my love,

TOBY'S REVENGE

Toby.

Printed in Great Britain
by Amazon